Over the Moon

COMPLETE PRIMARY ENGLISH LANGUAGE PROGRAM

Skills Book
2nd Class

LORRAINE LAWRANCE

GILL EDUCATION

Contents

Introduction

Over the Moon Programme – 2nd Class

There are 18 units of work in the *Over the Moon* Programme. Each unit covers a fortnight. Editable fortnightly plans (fully aligned with the Primary Language Curriculum) are available to download on GillExplore.

Reading Goals: A reading goal is attached to each unit in the readers to encourage self-monitoring.

Picture Books: Inspiring a love of literature is at the heart of *Over the Moon*. For each month, there is a carefully selected picture book that corresponds to one of the themes of the month. Explicit notes for teacher modelling are available in a Critical Thinking and Book Talk section of the *Teacher's Planning and Resource Book*.

Oral Language Posters: An Oral Language Poster is available for each month on GillExplore. The poster corresponds to one of the themes of the month and comes with games and activities.

Digital Library: Interact with *Over the Moon* through reader eBooks, phonics games, grammar exercises and much more.

Structure of the Skills Book

Before Reading: Brainstorm rich language for the upcoming text.

During Reading: Pause to engage in exciting 'book talk' activities.

After Reading: Consolidate learning through exercises designed to encourage independent thinking.

Comprehension: 'Text detective' exercises offer literal questions; 'digging deeper' exercises provide opportunities for inferential thinking; 'phrase finder' exercises explore vocabulary and phrases in the reader.

Phonics: Phonics are mapped to *Jolly Phonics* and are supported by dictation sentences, tongue-twisters and Literacy Station activities in the *Teacher's Planning and Resource Book*.

Grammar: Explicit examples lead the pupils through grammar exercises. These are enhanced in the Literacy Station activities for the fortnight.

Genre:
- Oral Genre – Engaging activities explore the five components of effective oral language.
- Writing Genre – *Over the Moon* follows the seven-step approach to teaching a writing genre.

Assessment: Fortnightly and termly assessments monitor children's learning. Running Records for readers are available along with a how-to guide. Resources to aid assessment, including pupil self-assessment, can be found in the *Teacher's Planning and Resource Book*.

Differentiation: Modified and extended activities are available so that children of different abilities can access and enjoy *Over the Moon*. Opportunities to write or draw responses to questions further aid differentiation.

Learning Outcomes: Learning Outcomes are listed on every page to show how the activities reflect the curriculum.

Icons: Icons serve as a visual guide to the approach required.

Group chat/ discussion	Pair chat/ discussion	Writing activity	Draw and/or colour	Text detective – literal questions	Digging deeper – inferential questions
Phrase finder/ word hunt	In-your-copy work	Take extra care with handwriting	**Free Writing:** Children colour one of these icons each time they have engaged in free writing (three times per week). See the Free Writing Topic Tree on the inside back cover for writing inspiration.		

Funny Bodies

Before Reading | **Brainstorming**

WALT: Talk about our bodies; match, describe and discuss images and captions.

 List all of the things that your body can do.

 A What strange things can people do with their bodies?

 B Caption each picture. Describe and discuss it.

Longest tongue	Stretchiest skin	Farthest eye pop
Longest hair	Longest nails	Most teeth

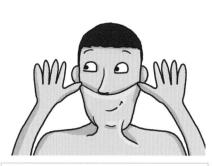

During Reading | **Book Talk**

WALT: Make connections; find important words; think about our senses.

 A Text-to-self connection: What does this story remind you of?

_____

B 🖊 Write key words from the text about each topic.

Boogers	Getting sick	Onions	Teeth
green glop	barfing	red	pearly whites
	germs	itchy	

 C What does an onion look, sound, smell, taste and feel like?

Looks: _____

Sounds: _____

Smells: _____

Tastes: _____

Feels: _____

Strand: Oral Language **Elements:** Communicating LO 3; Exploring and Using LO 9
Strand: Reading **Elements:** Communicating LO 1

After Reading | Understanding

A ✎ True or false?

Statement	True	False
1. Boogers keep your nose moist.		
2. Boogers protect your toes.		
3. Getting sick helps your body to get rid of bugs.		
4. Onions have a chemical that make your eyebrows itchy.		
5. A baby has 20 small teeth and an adult has 32 teeth.		

B 👥 Number the images to sequence them in the correct order.

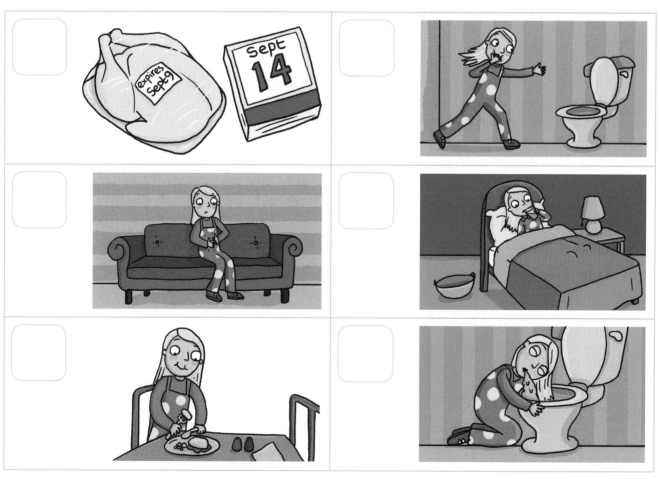

A 🔍 **Text detective**

1. What is Tom's favourite hobby?

_____

2. What is a booger?

_____

3. Why do we get sick?

_____

4. What are the orange bits in sick?

_____

5. What do onions have in them that make you cry?

_____

B **Digging deeper: Discuss.**

1. Why do you think Tom likes reading about funny bodies?

2. What might happen if we didn't have boogers inside our noses?

3. Why do you think babies are born without teeth?

4. How could you help your eyes while chopping onions?

5. What is an allergen?

6. Which topic did you find most interesting? Why?

C 🔭 **Phrase finder: Match each phrase to its meaning. Try to use the phrases in your free writing.**

1. come into contact with	crazy
2. off your rocker	don't forget this
3. bear this in mind	crying a lot
4. buckets of tears	to touch something or meet someone

Strand: Oral Language **Elements:** Understanding LO 6, 7; Exploring and Using LO 10
Strand: Reading **Elements:** Understanding LO 6; Exploring and Using LO 9

Phonics | **Silent b, Silent w**

WALT: Explore words with a silent 'b' or a silent 'w'.

A Say each word. Colour the silent 'b'. (Hint: A silent 'b' is found after the letter 'm' or before the letter 't'.)

bomb	comb	climb	crumb	debt	doubt	thumb
honeycomb		lamb	limb	numb	dumb	womb

B Fill in the blanks using the correct silent 'b' word above.

1. Ella likes to _____ her hair before she goes to bed.
2. Before you were born, you lived in your mother's _____.
3. "I _____ that it will rain today," said Mam.
4. Tom's favourite ice-cream flavour is _____.
5. Put your _____ up if you like cake!
6. Mary had a little _____. The poor lamb had a sore _____.

C Say each word. Colour the silent 'w' as you read it. (Hint: A silent 'w' is found before the letter 'r'.)

wrap	wren	wrong	wrench	write	wrinkle	wreck
written	answer	sword	wrist	two	wrestle	wriggle

D Ring the correct word in each sentence.

1. Dad has a **wrench / rench** in his toolkit.
2. Miss Teary has a deep **rinkle / wrinkle** on her forehead.
3. Baby Ed likes to **riggle / wriggle** about.
4. Ella had a chicken **rap / wrap** for her lunch.
5. Tom thinks it is cool to **wrestle / restle**.
6. A **wren / ren** has a tail that points up.

Strand: Reading **Element:** Understanding LO 4, 5
Strand: Writing **Element:** Understanding LO 4

5

A 👥 Colour all the words with a capital letter in Tom's diary entries. Say why each word takes a capital letter.

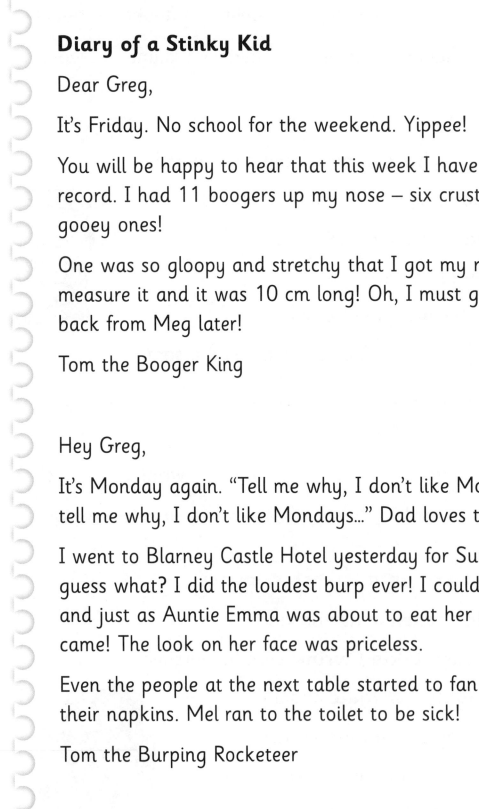

Diary of a Stinky Kid

Dear Greg,

It's Friday. No school for the weekend. Yippee!

You will be happy to hear that this week I have beaten my record. I had 11 boogers up my nose – six crusty ones and five gooey ones!

One was so gloopy and stretchy that I got my ruler out to measure it and it was 10 cm long! Oh, I must get that ruler back from Meg later!

Tom the Booger King

Hey Greg,

It's Monday again. "Tell me why, I don't like Mondays, tell me why, I don't like Mondays…" Dad loves that song.

I went to Blarney Castle Hotel yesterday for Sunday lunch and guess what? I did the loudest burp ever! I could feel it coming and just as Auntie Emma was about to eat her apple pie, out it came! The look on her face was priceless.

Even the people at the next table started to fan themselves with their napkins. Mel ran to the toilet to be sick!

Tom the Burping Rocketeer

Strand: Reading **Element:** Understanding LO 3
Strand: Writing **Element:** Understanding LO 3

Oral Genre | **Communicating**

A Talk about the strange things that your body does.

Topics

- What is a burp?
- What is earwax?
- Why do I get goosebumps?

- Why does sweat smell?
- Why does my nose run?
- Why do I shed skin?

B Voice jar: Re-read the text using one of the voices in the jar.

Why do onions make us cry?

It's a strange one! I'm sure most people don't feel sad when slicing up an onion. We don't cry when cutting up a carrot. So why does chopping an onion make us cry buckets of tears?

Onions contain a chemical (kem-i-kal). This chemical makes our eyes red and itchy. When an onion is cut, the chemical comes out of the onion. It then enters our eyes.

Our tear ducts (the holes in the small red triangles at the corners of our eyes) then make tears to flush out the chemical and clean our eyes.

A Plan an explanation piece on one of the topics you have read about.

Title (what it is about): _____

Statement/Introduction:

I want to explain _____

_____

Sequenced explanation:

(why/how) _____

_____

_____

(why/how) _____

_____

_____

(why/how) _____

_____

_____

Conclusion:

Now you can see why/how _____

because _____

_____

Strand: Writing Elements: Communicating LO 1; Exploring and Using LO 6, 7, 9

To the Art Exhibition

Before Reading | **Brainstorming**

WALT: Brainstorm and visualise.

✏️ **What inspires people to create art?**

(FW)

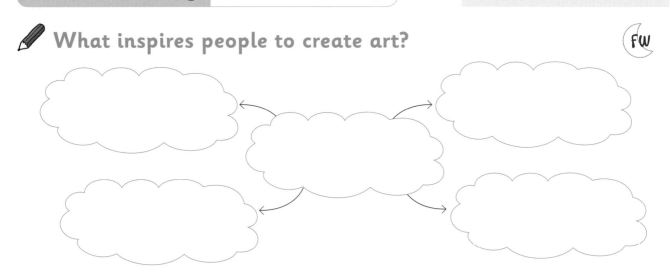

⭐ **A** 👥 **Choose an art form and try to explain it. Can you think of some more?**

sculpture	drawing	painting	fabric and fibre
printmaking			

⭐ **B** 👥 **What would you like to see in an art gallery?**

Strand: Oral Language **Element:** Communicating LO 2

9

A 🖊 **Answer in your own words. Choose key words to help you.**

Papier mâché	Marbling	Paper people
form, newspaper, paste, strips, layers, paint, decorate	oil paint, tray, water, floats, spoon, pattern, paper	symmetrical, cut, body parts, string, swing, paper fasteners

1. How does *papier mâché* work?

_____

_____

2. How does marbling work?

_____

_____

3. How do paper people work?

_____

_____

B **Explain what is happening in the image.**

I can see _____

_____

It seems _____

_____

I think that _____

_____

_____

It is clear _____

_____

Strand: Oral Language **Elements:** Communicating LO 2; Understanding LO 6
Strand: Reading **Element:** Exploring and Using LO 10
Strand: Writing **Element:** Exploring and Using LO 6

A 👥 Match each explanation piece snippet to the correct art form.

If the paint is too thick, it will not spread out nicely. If you add too much white spirit, the paint will become too watery.	Layers make the form more solid. If you do not have enough layers, you will be able to see through to the form.

Papier mâché

When water and oil mix, the oil floats to the top.	To make paper people, you need to be good at drawing the parts of the body.

Marbling

The form is the main part or the body.	Torn newspaper strips work better than cut strips. They make the object look smoother.

Paper people

They will allow the body parts to move and swing about. They need to be placed where the shoulders meet the arms and where the hips meet the legs.	Materials are things like newspaper, cardboard boxes, toilet-roll holders, pipe cleaners and milk carton tops.

After Reading | **Comprehension**

WALT: Recall information about the text and give our own opinions; explore phrases.

A **Text detective**

1. What does Ella do on Tuesdays?

_____

2. What will the children be doing soon?

_____

3. Why do you need torn newspaper strips for *papier mâché*?

_____

4. What happens when oil and water mix?

_____

5. What will paper fasteners allow the body parts to do?

_____

6. What do historians use paper dolls for?

_____

B **Digging deeper: Discuss.**

1. How do you think the girls feel about the art exhibition?

2. Why should you pay special attention to the two warning signs?

3. What might happen if you only used one layer of *papier mâché*?

4. Why is it important that the body parts are symmetrical?

5. Which would take the longest to do and why?

C   **Phrase finder: Match each phrase to its meaning.**

1. the best of buds	start from the beginning	
2. first things first	a small amount	
3. a taster	very good friends	

Strand: Oral Language **Elements:** Understanding LO 6; Exploring and Using LO 7, 10
Strand: Reading **Elements:** Understanding LO 6; Exploring and Using LO 9

| Phonics | Silent k, wh | Grammar | Capital Letters 2 |

WALT: Explore silent 'k', and 'wh' words; use capital letters.

 A Say each word. Colour the silent 'k' as you read it. (Hint: Silent 'k' is found before the letter 'n'.)

know	knot	knob	knuckle	knee	knit	knight
knife	kneel	knack	knocked	knead		knew

B Choose four silent 'k' words and write each in a sentence.

1. _____

2. _____

3. _____

4. _____

C Say each word. Colour 'wh' as you read it.

whale	wheat	wheel	wheelchair	whisper	white	whine
whistle	whirlpool	why	where	what	which	when

D Choose four 'wh' words and draw an image for each.

 E Colour all of the capital letters in the poster.

 Messy Hands Art Exhibition
Showing the work of Miss Evelyn's art students

Venue: Crawford Art Gallery   **Date:** September 28th

Papier mâché, fabric and fibre, painting, printing and much more.
There will also be a talk by the artist Evelyn Thomas
and a display of her work about recycled art.

Oral Genre | **Communicating**

FW

A Think outside the box! Discuss the topic in each box.

1. Paper is thin. Name three other things that are thin.	2. Balloons can float in the air. Name three other things that can float in the air.	3. Newspapers use ink. Name three other things that use ink.
4. Paste is sticky. Name three other things that are sticky.	5. Paint can be wet. Name three other things that are wet.	6. Dolls are toys. Name three other toys.
7. Oil floats on water. Name three other things that can float on water.	8. Paper fasteners hold things together. Name three other things that hold things together.	9. String can be long. Name three other things that are long.

B Give orders to your partner on how to design the paper doll's clothes.

Example: Place three pink stars on the hem of the skirt.

Strand: Oral Language **Elements:** Communicating LO 2; Understanding LO 6
Strand: Reading **Element:** Exploring and Using LO 6

Writing Genre | Exploring and Using

WALT: Use a template to plan and draft an explanation piece.

 Using the text in the reader to help you, plan and draft an explanation piece on how paper people work.

Title: _____

Statement (what paper people are):

_____

_____

Sequenced explanation (how they work):

(why/how)

_____

_____

(why/how)

_____

_____

_____

(why/how)

_____

_____

_____

Conclusion:

_____

_____

_____

A Making predictions while you read makes reading more exciting! Record your predictions.

Prediction from the title/cover/blurb: Compare how the paper dolls look on the front cover and the back cover.

I think that _____

_____

Prediction 1 during reading: What do you think will happen to the dolls when they meet the dinosaur, the tiger and the crocodile?

My guess is _____

_____

Prediction 2 during reading: What do you think will happen to the dolls when they meet the boy with scissors?

What might happen next is _____

_____

Prediction after reading: What will the mother and daughter do with the new paper dolls?

Now I think _____

_____

B What helped you to make your predictions? (FW)

When I read _____

I saw _____

I thought of _____

_____ made me think _____

Strand: Reading **Element:** Exploring and Using LO 9
Strand: Writing **Element:** Exploring and Using LO 6

The Wild Explorers

 What can you see, hear, smell, taste and touch when you read the title?

A Record the things that you expect to see on a nature walk.

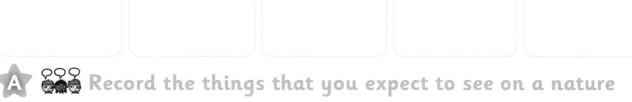

B How do you think these pictures were made?

I think _____

_____

_____

_____

_____

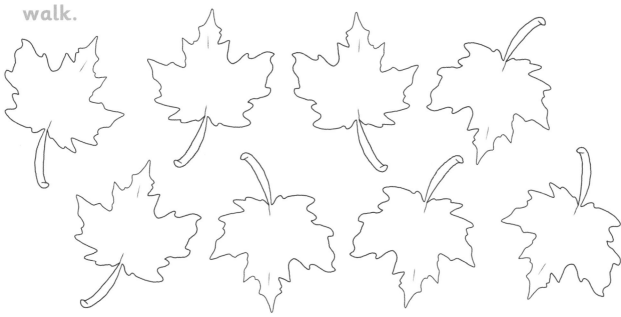

A Write what you already know, what you want to find out and what you have learned about each topic in the chart.

Topic	What I already know	What I want to find out	What I have learned
Leaves	Leaves grow on trees.	Why do leaves fall from trees in autumn?	
Trees			
Hedgehogs			
Grasshoppers			
Moths			
Beetles			

Strand: Oral Language **Element:** Exploring and Using LO 11, 12
Strand: Reading **Element:** Communicating LO 1

A Text detective

1. Where did the class go?

_____

2. What items were each group given?

_____

3. Which type of trees shed their leaves?

_____

4. How can you tell how old a tree is?

_____

5. Why do animals hibernate?

_____

6. Why do animals hibernate in winter, but not in summer?

_____

B   Digging deeper: Discuss.

1. Why do deciduous trees shed their leaves?

2. How do animals prepare for hibernation?

3. Why do hedgehogs curl up into a ball?

4. How do grasshoppers make noise?

5. Why does a tree have bark?

6. What other things might you see on a nature walk?

C Phrase finder: Fill in each sentence using your own idea.

1. I _____ just to be on the safe side.

2. We _____ just to be on the safe side.

3. You should _____ just to be on the safe side.

Strand: Oral Language **Elements:** Understanding LO 6; Exploring and Using LO 7, 10
Strand: Reading **Elements:** Understanding LO 6; Exploring and Using LO 9

19

Phonics | ph, ea | **Grammar** | **Verbs**

WALT: Explore 'ph' and 'ea' words; choose suitable verbs.

A Read each word. Colour 'ph' blue. Colour 'ea' red. Cover each word, spell it and then check it.

elephant	sphere	alphabet	dolphin	nephew
phone	pheasant	Philippines	atmosphere	autograph

bread	read	spread	thread	dead	head	breath
weather	feather	heavy	breakfast	treasure	pleasant

B Find the words that fit the shapes.

weather	thread	elephant	dolphin	phone	breakfast

Verbs are action (doing) words.

C Fill in the blanks using a suitable verb.

1. Ella and Tom _____ on a nature walk.

2. They _____ by bus and _____ songs all the way.

3. Ms Carol _____ a worksheet.

4. Deciduous trees _____ their leaves.

Strand: Reading **Element:** Understanding LO 3, 4, 5
Strand: Writing **Element:** Understanding LO 3, 4

Oral Genre **Communicating**

  Take turns explaining each of the following to your partner:

 FW

1. How a rubbing of tree bark is made

2. Why and how grasshoppers make noise

3. Why animals hibernate

4. Why and how hedgehogs protect themselves

B Discuss what you can see in these pictures of fireflies. What is happening and why?

mouse	bee	cockroach	ladybird	moth	earthworm
ant	fly	beetle	spider	wasp	woodlouse

Pest 😢	**Not a pest** 😃

Strand: Oral Language **Element:** Exploring and Using LO 11, 12
Strand: Writing **Element:** Communicating LO 2

21

Writing Genre | Exploring and Using

WALT: Use a template to plan and draft an explanation piece.

  Use the diagram to help you explain the life cycle of a ladybird.

1. Tiny yellow eggs are laid on leaves.

2. Then, each egg hatches into a larva after 7 days.

4. Finally, a pupa grows into a ladybird after 7 days.

3. Next, a larva grows into a pupa after 21 days.

Title: _____

Definition:

A ladybird is _____

How does it happen? (Explain each stage.)

First, tiny yellow eggs are _____

Then, each egg hatches into a _____ after _____ days.

Next, a larva grows into a _____ after _____ .

Finally, a pupa _____

Conclusion:

There are _____ stages in the life cycle of a _____ .

Strand: Oral Language **Element:** Exploring and Using LO 11
Strand: Writing **Element:** Exploring and Using LO 6, 7

My Little Book of Calm

✏️ **What does the title make you visualise?**

⭐ A 🗣️ **Talk about each activity and match it to an emotion.**

getting a present	🎁	😧 scared
seeing a monster	👾✏️	🙂 happy
playing with friends		🙂 proud
winning a prize	🏆	😃 excited
being teased		😢 sad

⭐ B 🗣️ **Design an emoji for each emotion.**   fw

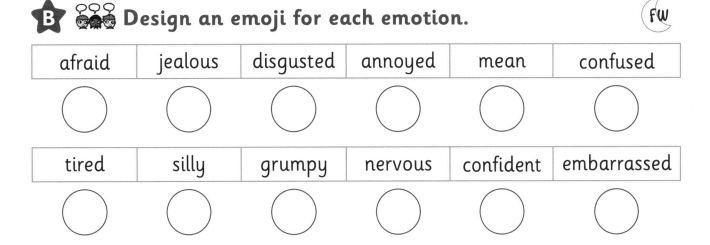

afraid	jealous	disgusted	annoyed	mean	confused
◯	◯	◯	◯	◯	◯

tired	silly	grumpy	nervous	confident	embarrassed
◯	◯	◯	◯	◯	◯

During Reading | **Book Talk**

WALT: Practise mindfulness and say how it makes us feel.

  Complete each activity and write how it makes you feel.

1. Place your hand on your stomach and take ten deep breaths. Pay attention to how your hand moves up and down while you breathe.

_____

2. Close your eyes and think about how you are feeling. Are you sad, happy, excited, scared or something else? Think about what tells you how you are feeling.

_____

3. Relax and sit very still. Pay attention to what you can see, hear, feel, taste and smell.

_____

4. Close your eyes for a minute and think about the happiest day of your life. Picture as many details as you can.

_____

5. Hold a small object such as a rubber or pencil in your hand. Notice the weight of it and what it feels like in your hand. You might notice something new about the object.

_____

6. Close your eyes for a minute and pay attention to how your clothing and shoes feel against your body. You might notice something new.

_____

Strand: Oral Language **Element:** Exploring and Using LO 10
Strand: Reading **Element:** Communicating LO 2

After Reading | **Understanding**

WALT: Recall top tips on how to be mindful; think of the feelings of others.

A Recall Ella's top tips on how to be mindful. Draw a picture and write a word or sentence to explain each.

1. Keep it simple.	2.	3.	4. Practise with a breathing buddy.
5. Make your walks mindful.	6.	7.	8.

B Let it go! Can you think of times when Ella might have felt angry, sad or nervous? Write them in the balloons.

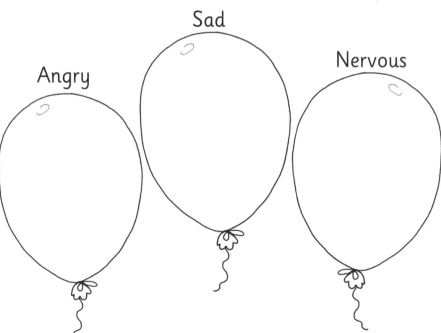

Angry

Sad

Nervous

Strand: Oral Language **Element:** Exploring and Using LO 8, 10
Strand: Reading **Element:** Exploring and Using LO 9

After Reading | Comprehension

WALT: Recall information about the text and give our own opinions; study words.

A 🔍 **Text detective**

1. How does Ella feel most of the time?

2. What happens to her sometimes?

3. What has she been learning about?

4. What does she have at bedtime?

5. What kinds of food does she eat?

6. What is a noticing walk?

  Digging deeper: Discuss.

1. What makes Ella worry?
2. How does breathing help you to be calm?
3. Why do you think the word 'breathe' is repeated in each tip?
4. What would your personal weather report say today?
5. How does a breathing buddy work?
6. What does the phrase 'don't be a couch potato' mean?
7. How can you practise mindfulness at home?

 👀 **Word study: Choose a bold word in the text and complete the following:**

1. Write it in three different colours.   2. Draw a picture of it.

3. Read, cover, remember and spell it.   4. Put it into a sentence.

Strand: Oral Language **Elements:** Understanding LO 5, 6; Exploring and Using LO 7
Strand: Reading **Element:** Exploring and Using LO 9
Strand: Writing **Element:** Understanding LO 4

Phonics **Soft c, Soft g**

A Read the rhyme. Colour the soft 'c' as you read it. (Hint: The letter 'c' says 's' when followed by 'i', 'e' or 'y'.)

Are there cereal and spices in outer space?

Do space people run a fancy-dress race?

Who has gone to space, other than mice?

Can aliens trace the word 'cylinder' twice?

B Fill in the blanks using the correct soft 'c' word.

space	slice	celery	juice	practice	cereal

1. Ella had a bowl of _____ and a glass of _____ for breakfast.

2. Mam uses _____ to make vegetable soup.

3. My niece would like a _____ of cake.

4. Would you fancy going to outer _____?

5. _____ makes perfect.

 C Say each word. Colour the soft 'g' as you read it. (Hint: The letter 'g' says 'j' when followed by 'i', 'e' or 'y'.)

gel	allergy	ginger	gym	gentle	genie	giant	cage
gem	bridge	gerbil	age	giraffe	Egypt	fragile	magic

D Ring the correct word(s) in each sentence.

1. Tom has an **allergy** / **allerjy** to dust.

2. Baby Ed's favourite animal is a **jiraffe** / **giraffe**.

3. Can I put my teacher in a **caje** / **cage**?

4. Grandad walked across the **bridge** / **bridje**.

5. I would like to visit **Ejypt** / **Egypt**.

6. The beautiful **gem** / **jem** is very **frajile** / **fragile**.

Grammar | Alphabetical Order

WALT: Put words in alphabetical order.

If you are writing a list of words in alphabetical order and there are two or more words that begin with the same letter, check the second letter.

Example: calm and **cheerful** both start with '**c**', but we know that '**a**' comes before '**h**', so **calm** comes before **cheerful**.

A In your copy, write each list of words in alphabetical order.

1. Happy words	2. Sad words	3. Annoyed words
glad	disappointed	furious
confident	lonely	mean
delighted	ashamed	irritated
terrific	unloved	disgusted
loved	sorry	fuming
calm	miserable	frustrated
proud	awful	mad
cheerful	worried	violent
excited	hurt	grumpy
content	unhappy	
relaxed	gloomy	
thankful		
silly		

28

Strand: Reading **Element:** Understanding LO 3
Strand: Writing **Element:** Understanding LO 3

A 🖉 **Signpost the genre of explanation using the labels in the word box.**

title	statement	explanation	concluding comment

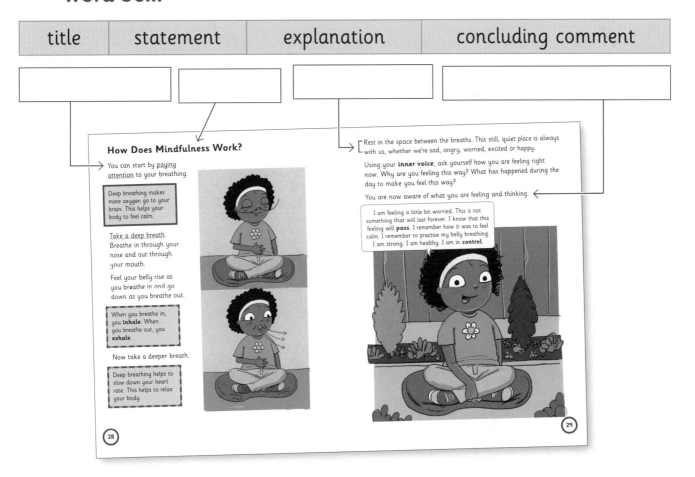

How Does Mindfulness Work?

You can start by paying attention to your breathing.

Deep breathing makes more oxygen go to your brain. This helps your body to feel calm.

Take a deep breath. Breathe in through your nose and out through your mouth.

Feel your belly rise as you breathe in and go down as you breathe out.

When you breathe in, you **inhale**. When you breathe out, you **exhale**.

Now take a deeper breath.

Deep breathing helps to slow down your heart rate. This helps to relax your body.

Rest in the space between the breaths. This still, quiet place is always with us, whether we're sad, angry, worried, excited or happy.

Using your **inner voice**, ask yourself how you are feeling right now. Why are you feeling this way? What has happened during the day to make you feel this way?

You are now aware of what you are feeling and thinking.

I am feeling a little bit worried. This is not something that will last forever. I know that this feeling will **pass**. I remember how it was to feel calm. I remember to practise my belly breathing. I am strong. I am healthy. I am in **control**.

28

29

 B 👥 **Take turns explaining each of the following to your partner.**

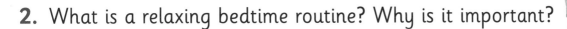

1. What is a noticing walk?

2. What is a relaxing bedtime routine? Why is it important?

3. What does it mean to be a mindful eater? How can you be one?

4. What is buddy breathing?

 C 📖 **Draft an explanation piece on how to be calm. Insert a title, an introduction, why/how and a conclusion. Swap your work with your partner. Give each other a star and a wish for your work.**

Strand: Oral Language **Element:** Exploring and Using LO 8
Strand: Reading **Element:** Communicating LO 2
Strand: Writing **Element:** Exploring and Using LO 6, 7, 8

Good readers make connections as they read! Making connections is looking for similarities between things.

 What does this book remind you of?

> I breathe slowly in,
> I breathe slowly out. My breath
> is a pathway of peace
> moving softly through me.
> Each day I can breathe and be.

This reminds me of

> How I rush rush rush!
> Thoughts flutter and dart like birds.
> Slow down, thoughts.
> Come quietly with me.
> There is time to breathe and be.

This reminds me of

> I watch the stream.
> Each thought is a floating leaf.
> One leaf is worry,
> another leaf is sadness.
> The leaves drift softly away.

This reminds me of

Strand: Oral Language **Element:** Exploring and Using LO 8, 10
Strand: Reading **Element:** Exploring and Using LO 9

A Day in the Life of Tom's Shoe

| Before Reading | Brainstorming |

WALT: Sort objects into categories; think about what shoes do every day.

 What words come to mind when you read the title?

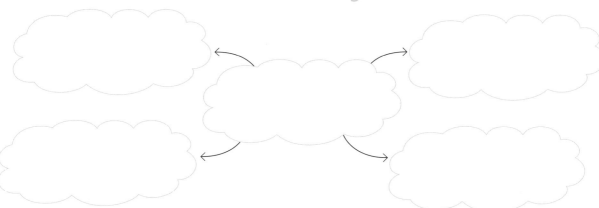

A Sort the shoes into piles! FW

| boots | sandals | flip-flops | runners | loafers |
| wellies | pumps | high heels | slippers | clogs |

Summer pile	Winter pile	All-year-round pile

B Record all of the places your shoes go with you.

Strand: Oral Language **Element:** Exploring and Using LO 8, 9
Strand: Writing **Element:** Understanding LO 5

During Reading | Book Talk

A **What was Tom's shoe thinking at each of these points?**

1. Tom left him lying on the cold kitchen floor all night.

2. He saw Meg and Mel's shoes all neatly lined up.

3. He saw Tom was wearing the same pair of socks for the whole week.

4. Tom's verruca was rubbing against him.

5. He was snuggled up beside the radiator at school.

6. He was chatting to his friends.

7. Tom was playing soccer.

8. He was covered in mud and dog poo.

9. He heard Mam say that Tom would get a new pair of shoes.

Strand: Reading **Element:** Exploring and Using LO 7

WALT: Make predictions; compare new and old objects.

 What do you predict happened to Tom's shoe when he 'retired'?

_____

 Compare Tom's old shoe with a new shoe, using the vocabulary below. Can you add suitable words of your own?

trendy	comfy	shiny	old	clean	dirty	worn
fancy	holey	falling apart		top-of-the-line		uncomfortable

Old shoe	New shoe

List the things that Tom could have done to take better care of his shoes.

1. Place them neatly on the shoe rack.

2. _____

3. _____

4. _____

After Reading | Comprehension

WALT: Recall information about the text and give our own opinions; explore phrases.

  A Text detective

1. What was Tom doing last night?

2. What did Tom have on the skin of his foot?

3. Where did the teacher move Tom's desk?

4. Which sport did Tom play outside?

5. What type of shoe is Tom's shoe?

  B Digging deeper: Discuss.

1. Why do you think Tom did not change his socks all week?

2. Why was the shoe jealous of Meg and Mel's shoes?

3. How do you think Tom felt when he stepped in the dog poo?

4. Objects don't have feelings. Think about how other objects might feel if they did have feelings.

5. What was Mam's reaction when she saw Tom's shoe?

6. What sort of retirement did the shoe think he was going to have?

C Phrase finder: In your copy, write each phrase in a sentence to show its meaning.

fw

1. I couldn't believe my eyes

2. green with envy

3. a hard-knock life

4. raining cats and dogs

5. the least of my worries

6. every cloud has a silver lining

Strand: Oral Language **Elements:** Understanding LO 6; Exploring and Using LO 7, 10
Strand: Reading **Elements:** Understanding LO 6; Exploring and Using LO 9

Phonics | wa, ou

WALT: Explore 'wa' and 'ou' words.

A  Read the rhyme. Colour 'wa' as you read it.

Wally the walrus wanders over to the water

to watch the swan wading in the water.

When Wally wanders over to the water,

the swan wanders off into the swamp.

B   Fill in the blanks using the correct 'wa' word.

washing	water	wad	wasp	swan	watch	wallet

1. The _____ flew into the flower.

2. When I am thirsty, I drink _____.

3. Mam hung the _____ on the line.

4. Dad had a big _____ of cash in his _____.

5. Come and _____ the fireworks.

6. A _____ is a type of bird.

C   Say each word. Colour 'ou' as you read it.

about	crouch	found	bounce	cloud	round	loud
ground	sprout	proud	mouth	ouch	south	house

D   Ring the correct word in each sentence.

1. Tom **found** / **fownd** a mouse in his house.

2. Grandad has been to the **Sowth** / **South** Pole.

3. Lainey likes to **bounce** / **bunce** on the trampoline.

4. There is a rain **clud** / **cloud** in the sky.

5. Ella had an ulcer in her **mooth** / **mouth**.

6. There were six Brussels **spruts** / **sprouts** on my plate.

Grammar | Doubling Rule

| If a word has:
one vowel
one final consonant
that is not w, x or y | → | Double the final consonant and add 'ing'.
Examples:
run → run**ning**   fit → fit**ting**
skip → skip**ping**   hug → hug**ging** |

A   Sort these verbs under the headings below.

| shop | jump | sit | play | saw | stop | train | swim |
| skip | stamp | clap | step | stand | sing | hop | look |

Double letters +ing	Single letter +ing
shopping	jumping

B   Fill in the blanks.

| trailing | brushing | clapping | running | swimming | stamping |

1. Tom went _____ in his new shoes.

2. Baby Ed started _____ when he saw his mam.

3. Lainey started _____ lessons.

4. The snail was _____ slime along the ground.

5. Ella was _____ her hair upstairs.

6. Evan was _____ his foot, because he was angry.

Strand: Reading Element: Understanding LO 3
Strand: Writing Element: Understanding LO 3

Take turns talking about some recent events in your life. Use the prompts below to help you.

Examples: a birthday party, a holiday, an accident or a trip to the cinema, zoo or sports centre

When

What day?

What time?

When did this event take place?

Who

Who did you go with?

Who did you play with?

Who else was there?

What

What did you do?

What happened next?

What did you like most?

Where

Where did you go?

Where did it happen?

Where were you after that?

Why

Why did you go there?

Why did you do that?

Why did that happen?

Feeling

How did it make you feel?

Why did you feel that way?

Writing Genre | **Exploring and Using**

A Draft a recount about one of the events you discussed with your partner.

| When did it happen? | Who was there? | What did you do? |
| Where did it happen? | Why did that happen? | How did you feel? |

On

First,

Next,

Then,

Finally,

Strand: Writing **Element:** Exploring and Using LO 6, 7, 9

#STORMOPHELiA

| Before Reading | Brainstorming |

WALT: Make predictions; visualise; ask questions.

 What can you see, hear, smell, taste and touch when you read the title?

 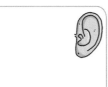  

A **Word weaver: The words below appear in the text in this order.**

| storm | battered | travel | power | killed | roof | damage |

1. Predict what this recount text might be about.   fw

I predict that _____

_____

2. What question do you have?

_____

B **Sneak preview: Read this snippet from the text.**

> One woman died after the car she was travelling in was struck by a falling tree in Waterford.

1. Add to your prediction using the new information you have read.

Now, I predict that _____

_____

2. What new question do you have?

_____

Fill in the KWL chart using information from the text.

What I already know ❮K❯	What I want to find out ❮W❯	What I have learned ❮L❯
Storms bring wind and rain.	What damage did the storm do?	

B **Think sheet: Complete each sentence as you read the text. Say what made you choose each point.**

I'm thinking

I'm noticing

I'm wondering

I'm feeling

I'm surprised by

I'm confused by

Strand: Oral Language Element: Exploring and Using LO 11
Strand: Reading Element: Exploring and Using LO 9

After Reading **Understanding**

WALT: Use the five Ws to find important points in the text.

  A Write important points for each of the five Ws.

When	Who	What

Where	Why

B Draw and label a picture showing what happened during the storm. (fw)

After Reading | **Comprehension**

WALT: Recall information about the text and give our own opinions; explore phrases.

A **Text detective**

1. In Kerrypike National School, what has been replaced? By what?

2. What did Tom and Ella look up to help them with their project?

3. When did Storm Ophelia hit Ireland?

4. What were many homes left without?

5. How many people died during Storm Ophelia?

B **Digging deeper: Discuss.**

1. What do you think is the worst thing about a storm?

2. Why might a home project be better than homework?

3. How do you think people were affected by the travel disruption?

4. What things could you <u>not</u> do without water?

5. Why was Tom dragging his finger along the window?

6. What kinds of games would you play if you had no electricity?

C   **Phrase finder: Match each phrase to its meaning.**

1. give it a shot	wait a minute	
2. smashed and bashed	destroyed	
3. vanished into thin air	have a go	
4. hold your horses	disappeared	

Strand: Oral Language **Elements:** Understanding LO 6; Exploring and Using LO 7, 10
Strand: Reading **Elements:** Understanding LO 6; Exploring and Using LO 9

Phonics | **air, ch** | **Grammar** | **Past Tense Verbs**

WALT: Explore 'air' and 'ch' words; explore past tense 'ed' verbs.

A Read each word. Colour 'air' green. Colour 'ch' yellow. Cover each word, spell it and then check it.

pair	dairy	chair	air	hairy	hairbrush	airport
stairs	repair	fairy	lair	unfair	fairground	aircraft

chain	charm	chess	choose	punch	pouch	match
chase	cheese	chop	church	bench	peach	torch

B Choose two 'ai' and two 'ch' words and draw a picture of each.

The letters '**ed**' at the end of a verb tell us that it is in the **past tense**. The past tense tells us about things that have already happened.

C Word hunt: Find these past tense verbs in the text and write the page number.

upgraded ⬜   bashed ⬜   smashed ⬜   killed ⬜

vanished ⬜   looked ⬜   started ⬜   hoped ⬜

D In your copy, write each past tense verb above in a sentence to show its meaning. (fw)

A **Retell the main events in the text using the word box.**

First	Next	Then	Finally

B 🖉 **Label each piece of information with one or more of the five Ws (when, who, what, where and why).**

Information	Which W?
1. It was the worst storm in Ireland for 50 years.	
2. On Monday October 16th, 2017, a storm began to brew in Ireland.	
3. There was a lot of travel disruption.	
4. Schools and businesses were closed for days on end.	
5. Around 330,000 homes were left without power.	
6. Many homes had no water, because the pipes burst.	
7. No electricity meant no lights, TV, tablets or phones.	
8. Three people died because of the storm.	
9. One woman died after the car she was travelling in was struck by a falling tree in Waterford.	
10. A man was killed while clearing a fallen tree with a chainsaw in Tipperary. Another man died in Louth after a tree fell on his car.	
11. The storm caused lots and lots of damage.	

Strand: Oral Language Element: Exploring and Using LO 11
Strand: Reading Element: Exploring and Using LO 9

🖉 **Plan and draft your own recount using the examples in the recount writing mat to help you.**

When	Who	What	Where	Why
Monday	friend	read	town	birthday
Saturday	Mam	played	café	holiday
last weekend	Dad	watched	beach	fun
last month	sister	ate	park	reward

Past tense verbs	Written in the first person (I, we)		
First	Next	Then	Finally

Title:	
Orientation: (when, who, what, where, why)	
Events: (First, Next, Then, Finally)	
Conclusion:	

Questioning helps us to dig deeper into the text.

 A Fill in the clouds of wonder with questions about *Storm Whale.*

I wonder if Noi has a mam.
I wonder how Noi feels when
his dad goes off to work.
I wonder what the storm left behind.
I wonder what Noi saw in the distance.

FW

Strand: Reading **Element:** Exploring and Using LO 9
Strand: Writing **Element:** Understanding LO 3

Pen Pals

Before Reading **Brainstorming**

WALT: Visualise, make predictions and make connections.

 What is a pen pal?

A Word weaver: The words below appear in the text. Can you predict what it will be about?

Advent wreath	decorations	carols	lantern festival	star
neureos	turkey	email	panto	banana trees	Mumbai

B Tom's pen pal lives in India. What comes to mind when you think of India?

C Text-to-self connection: What do you do at Christmas?

My Christmas Traditions

_____

_____

_____

WALT: Examine differences between Christmas in Ireland and in Mumbai; examine things in order.

A **List the differences between Christmas in Ireland and in Mumbai.** (fw

Christmas in Ireland ▮▮	Christmas in Mumbai

B 🖊 **How did Aarav make the paper lantern?**

First, _____

Next, _____

_____

Then, _____

_____

Finally, _____

C **Draw and label what Tom eats for Christmas dinner.**

First: starter	Next: main course	Finally: dessert

Strand: Oral Language **Element:** Understanding LO 6
Strand: Reading **Element:** Exploring and Using LO 7

After Reading | **Comprehension**

A **Text detective**

1. Where did Tom meet Aarav?

2. How many candles are there on an Advent wreath?

3. What do Tom's nana and grandad have for dessert at Christmas?

4. What do they call Christmas in Mumbai?

5. Why do they hang the lanterns between the houses in Mumbai?

B **Digging deeper: Discuss.**

1. Why do you think Ms Carol put all of the things for making the Advent wreaths at different tables?

2. What do you notice about how Tom and Aarav greet each other?

3. How are *neureos* made?

4. Why do you think banana trees are decorated for Christmas in Mumbai?

5. Why is the *Late Late Toy Show* so popular?

6. Would you like to visit another country for Christmas? Why/Why not?

7. Why do different countries have different traditions?

C **Word study: Choose three bold words in the text and complete the following for each:**

1. Write it in three different colours.
2. Draw a picture of it.
3. Read, cover, remember and spell it.
4. Put it into a sentence.

Strand: Oral Language **Elements:** Understanding LO 5, 6; Exploring and Using LO 7
Strand: Reading **Element:** Exploring and Using LO 9
Strand: Writing **Element:** Understanding LO 4

| Phonics | ai, ee | Grammar | Irregular Verbs 1 |

WALT: Explore 'ai' and 'ee' words; write irregular verbs in the past tense.

 A 🖊 Sort the 'ai' words and 'ee' words. Write them using three different colours as in the examples.

Lainey	wheel	need	remain	three	again	cheek
wait	sheep	queen	sheets	portrait	trail	agree

'ai' words	'ee' words
Lainey	wheel

> **Irregular verbs** do not take 'ed' in the past tense.
> **Examples:** "I **wrote** (write) a letter to my pen pal," **said** (say) Tom.

B 🖊 Write each irregular verb in the past tense using the word bank to help you. (fw

broke	taught	heard	gave	stood	rode	hid
grew	fed	wrote	felt	swept	stung	slept
stole	shook	bit	said	fought	woke	built

grow _____	break _____	ride _____
hear _____	bite _____	stand _____
feed _____	teach _____	give _____
sweep _____	feel _____	sting _____
say _____	steal _____	sleep _____
wake _____	build _____	shake _____
hide _____	fight _____	write _____

Strand: Reading **Element:** Understanding LO 3, 4, 5
Strand: Writing **Element:** Understanding LO 3, 4, 5

Choose a topic from the topic tree. Prepare an oral story about your topic, using the word box.

First	Next	Then	Finally

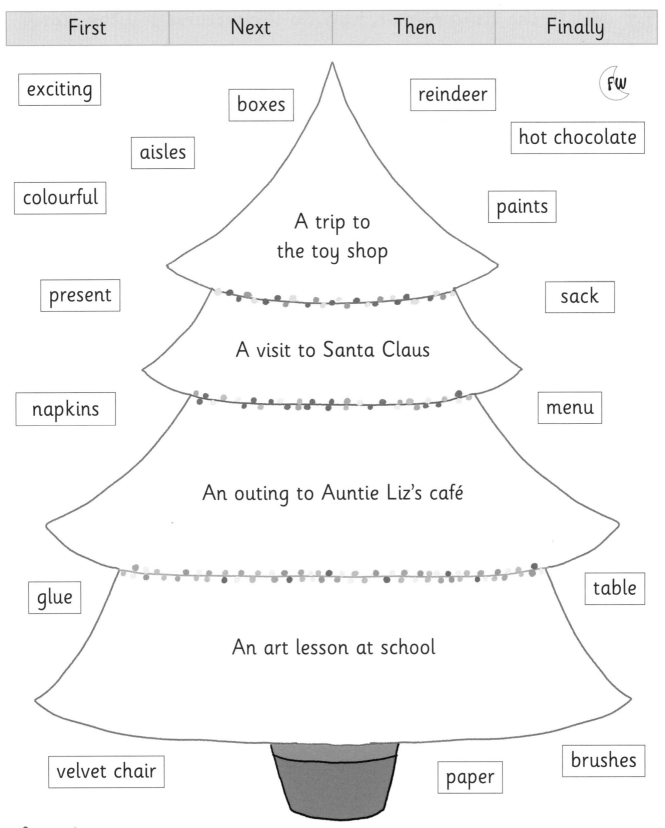

exciting

boxes

reindeer

FW

hot chocolate

aisles

colourful

A trip to the toy shop

paints

present

sack

A visit to Santa Claus

napkins

menu

An outing to Auntie Liz's café

glue

table

An art lesson at school

velvet chair

paper

brushes

B **Write a recount about one of the topics from the topic tree.**

Picture Book | Visualising

Visualising is when you create images using words or details from the book.

A 👥 In the story *Mirror*, how do the pictures tell the story? Talk about the textures that are used in the book. ⌒fw

B ✏️ Can you draw an image from Australia and an image from Morocco? Explain how they are different.

Australia

Morocco

_____

_____

_____

_____

Strand: Oral Language **Element:** Understanding LO 6
Strand: Reading **Element:** Exploring and Using LO 9

A Merry Messi Christmas Play

Before Reading	Brainstorming

WALT: Brainstorm; make and compare lists; make requests.

✏️ What words come to mind when you read the title?

A 🗣️ Make a list of all the things that you do on Christmas Eve. Discuss and compare lists with your partner.

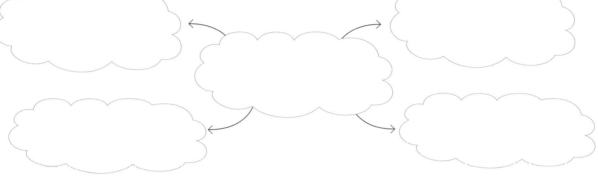

'Twas the night before Christmas...

_____

_____

_____

B 🗣️ It is important to use manners when asking for something. How will you ask Santa for gifts? How can you thank him? FW

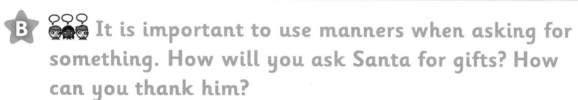

Asking: Dear Santa,

_____

_____

_____

_____

Thanking: Dear Santa,

_____

_____

_____

_____

During Reading **Book Talk**

WALT: Answer questions from a character's point of view; make predictions.

⭐ Read each snippet from the text and answer the questions.

Narrator 1: He said he's not going to deliver the presents this year. He has lost the plot! We're in utter despair!

1. Why does Santa not want to deliver the presents?

_____

_____

_____

Narrator 1: At headquarters, the Elf Inspectors are checking toys and going berserk. All the poor elves are tired from their hard work.

2. What questions do the Elf Inspectors have?

_____

_____

_____

Santa: I've a plateful of cookies and a jugful of milk. I feel so relaxed and my skin feels like silk.

3. Will Santa change his mind? Will the children get their presents? What do you predict will happen to Christmas?

_____

_____

_____

Strand: Oral Language **Elements:** Communicating LO 1; Exploring and Using LO 7
Strand: Reading **Elements:** Understanding LO 3; Exploring and Using LO 10

After Reading | Understanding

WALT: Make connections to the text; visualise items; make predictions; draw and label.

 A 🖊 Read each snippet from the text and answer the questions.

> **Messi:** You can't cancel Christmas. It's too important you see. You were the one who gave me my first football at the age of three.

1. What were some of your favourite presents that you got from Santa? Why? List and draw them.

    _____

    _____

    _____

    _____

    _____

> **Narrator 1:** Rudolph had been eating too many cakes, so he just wasn't able...

2. What do you predict Rudolph's new diet will look like? Draw and label it.

After Reading **Comprehension**

A  **Text detective**

1. What night was it?

_____

2. Why did Elf Kevin come to the Mooneys' house?

_____

3. What was wrong with Santa?

_____

4. Why were the elves going berserk?

_____

5. What plan did Ella come up with?

_____

6. What did Santa decide to do?

_____

B   **Digging deeper: Discuss.**

1. How do you know that Ella is good with technology?

2. Why do you think Rudolph changed his diet?

3. Explain this joke from the play: Right, how is the yo-yo department doing? – A bit up and down, but we're getting there.

4. How did Santa get addicted to Sky?

C **Phrase finder: Match each phrase to its meaning by colouring them both the same. You will need four colours.**

crying my eyes out	skin feels like silk	crying lots of tears	keep on your hat
don't overreact	gone crazy	lost the plot	a smooth feel to the skin

Strand: Oral Language **Elements:** Understanding LO 6; Exploring and Using LO 7, 10
Strand: Reading **Elements:** Understanding LO 6; Exploring and Using LO 9

Phonics **ie, oa**

A Read the rhyme. Colour 'ie' as you read it.

She cries when she sees flies.

She cries when she eats fries.

She cries and cries when she tells lies.

She cries when she bakes pies.

B Fill in the blanks using the correct 'ie' word.

tried	cried	tie	pie	untie	flies

1. Dad wears a shirt and _____ to work.

2. I cannot wait to _____ the bow on my present.

3. "Anything for you, Messi," Santa _____.

4. Rudolph _____ at the front of Santa's sleigh.

5. Please leave out a mince _____ on Christmas Eve.

6. I _____ to stay awake but I fell asleep.

C Read each word. Colour 'oa' as you read it.

goat	soap	oak	foal	oatmeal	upload	float
throat	railroad	coach	moan	approach	toast	coal

D Cross out the nonsense words. Use the words above to help you.

cout	goat	towst	boat	float
sok	cach	coat	bloat	toast
cloak	lof	pbloat	gloak	roam
coach	load	soak	loaf	lowd

Irregular verbs do not take 'ed' in the past tense.
Examples:

Present:	swim	buy	sell	fly	run	drink	go
Past:	swam	bought	sold	flew	ran	drank	went

Present:	freeze	eat	write	speak	blow	fall	sleep
Past:	froze	ate	wrote	spoke	blew	fell	slept

A 🖉 **Fill in the blanks using the correct past tense verb.**

1. The lake (freeze) _____ on Christmas Eve.

2. Tom (write) _____ his letter to Santa.

3. Santa (drink) _____ the glass of milk that I left out.

4. Lainey and Ava (sleep) _____ in the same room.

5. Nana (buy) _____ me a new jumper for Christmas.

6. I (blow) _____ out the candle on the advent wreath.

7. Tom (run) _____ down the stairs on Christmas morning.

8. We (eat) _____ turkey, ham and potatoes on Christmas Day.

B 🎄 **Play bingo. Your teacher will call out the irregular verbs.**

B	I	N	G	O
buy	blow	come	eat	do
draw	sing	begin	get	know
bring	hang	**Free Space**	grow	drink
make	give	run	catch	meet
read	send	hear	say	go

Strand: Reading **Element:** Understanding LO 3
Strand: Writing **Element:** Understanding LO 3

Oral Genre | **Communicating**

WALT: Talk about our own experience; label parts of a recount.

A Talk about your visit to Santa.

B ✏️ Label parts of this recount with 'when', 'who', 'what', 'where' and 'why'.

My Visit to Santa

Yesterday my family and I went to visit Santa Claus in Westport House. We travelled there by train. When we got to the entrance, we showed the elf our tickets. The elf gave us stickers with our names on them and some reindeer food.

We went into the first room. It was called 'Polar Express'. The room was dark and my baby brother started to cry. Mam fed him to calm him down. We saw three polar bears and lots of snow. There was a train in the room too. The elf told us to jump aboard. The train brought us into the next room.

The next room was called 'Elves' Post Office'. The elves were busy sorting out letters to Santa. They had a list of who was naughty and nice. We were on the good list. Woo hoo! We got a shock when the reindeers arrived with a sleigh to take us to the next room. On the way, we passed more elves, busy making toys in the workshop.

Finally, we got to Santa's grotto. Santa was sitting in a red velvet chair. We took turns sitting on his knee and he asked us what we would like for Christmas. He told us to be extra good at home and to leave out a carrot and water for the reindeer and some milk and cookies for him. We got our photo taken. We had a lovely day.

Strand: Oral Language **Element:** Exploring and Using LO 7
Strand: Reading **Element:** Exploring and Using LO 10

59

A Read the song lyrics. Write a recount in which Santa is telling Mrs Claus about the time he got stuck up the chimney. Discuss your writing with your partner.

When Santa Got Stuck up the Chimney

When Santa got stuck up the chimney,

He began to shout,

"You girls and boys won't get any toys,

If you don't pull me out.

There's soot on my back,

And my beard is all black.

My nose is tickling too!"

When Santa got stuck up the chimney,

"Achoo, achoo, achoo!"

| When: _____ |
| Who: _____ |
| What: _____
 _____ |
| Where: _____ |
| Why: _____
 _____ |
| How: _____
 _____ |

Strand: Writing **Element:** Exploring and Using LO 6, 7

The Blizzard of 1947

| Before Reading | Brainstorming |

WALT: Put words into alphabetical order; describe the weather.

 What can you see, hear, smell, taste and touch when you read the title?

 A What weather words do you know? List them alphabetically.

a	b	c	d	e	f
g	h	i	j	k	l
m	n	o	p	q	r
s	t	u	v	w	x
y	z				

B Take turns at being a weather forecaster describing today's weather. Use the prompts below.

- The sky looks...
- Be sure to...
- The air feels...
- Lately it has been...
- This is because...
- People are wearing...
- I expect that...

A ✏️ Fill in the clouds of wonder with questions about the text.

B 👥 Text-to-text connection: Does this story remind you of another reader in this series? How?

C 🖍️ Draw what you can visualise from reading page 71 on the left and from page 74 on the right. Describe what you have drawn.

After Reading **Understanding**

WALT: Find very important points in the text; justify chosen points.

 🖊 **Determining importance: Create an index for important points in the text by finding the page numbers.**

1. Ella and Tom win a competition   page _____

2. Ella and Tom go to Dublin   page _____

3. Ella and Tom report on the blizzard of 1947   page _____

4. Snow begins to fall in Ireland on February 24th   page _____

5. Children playing, having fun   page _____

6. People burn items to keep warm   page _____

7. Postmen become like weather prophets   page _____

8. Crops and animals perish   page _____

9. Céilí dancing on the frozen lake   page _____

10. Many people die   page _____

11. What inspired Ella and Tom   page _____

FW

  🖊 **Complete the 3, 2, 1 chart.**

Write three important points in the text.

1. _____

2. _____

3. _____

Write two interesting facts in the text.

1. _____

2. _____

Write one question you have that has not been answered.

_____

After Reading | **Comprehension**

WALT: Recall information about the text and give our own opinions; explore phrases.

  A **Text detective**

1. Where are Tom and Ella going and what will they do there?

2. What were people looking forward to doing in the snow?

3. On which lake did the local people dance?

4. Who made weather predictions?

5. For how long did the snow linger on?

6. What was Storm Emma also known as?

  B **Digging deeper: Discuss.**

1. How do you know that Tom and Ella are good friends?

2. Why do you think the blizzard was described as the 'coldest and harshest in living memory'?

3. What would you have done if you had lived on a farm during the blizzard?

4. How is life different now compared to life in 1947?

C  **Phrase finder: Match each phrase to its meaning.**

1. ants in our pants	two people who are very alike
2. two peas in a pod	from house to house
3. from pillar to post	stopped
4. ground to a halt	feeling restless

Strand: Oral Language **Elements:** Understanding LO 6; Exploring and Using LO 7, 10
Strand: Reading **Elements:** Understanding LO 6; Exploring and Using LO 9

Say each word. Colour 'ue' as you read it.

true	argue	rescue	tissue	statue	Tuesday	continue
blue	cruel	avenue	glue	value	barbecue	blueberry

  Ring the correct word(s) in each sentence.

1. It is **true / trew** that Lainey likes the colour **blue / blew**?

2. Ella and Tom walked down the **avenyew / avenue**.

3. Please don't **argue / argyu** with your mam.

4. Miss Evelyn needs some more **gloo / glue**.

5. There is a **statue / stattue** in my garden.

6. Please pass me a **tuessie / tissue**.

  Say each word. Colour the /k/ sound as you hear it.

magic	leek	break	public	music	comic	soak	speak
steak	park	creak	panic	cook	seek	hook	cheek

 Examine the /k/ sound words above.

1. Which vowels come before a 'c' ending? _____

2. Which vowels come before a 'k' ending? _____

 Fill in the blanks using the correct /k/ sound word.

1. How many times a day do your eyes _____?

2. Baby Ed went on the swing in the _____.

3. The stink from a _____ is revolting!

4. Nan gave me a kiss on the _____.

5. Mrs Lynch wanted to _____ to Evan's mam.

6. "Do not _____ the window with that sliotar," said Dad.

WALT: Sort nouns into categories.

 A Roll a die. When you land on a word, say what type of noun it is.

Types of nouns: person place animal thing

 FW

Start	boy	school	**Move forward 3 places.**	competition	pea

Miss a turn.

snowman	**Miss a turn.**	snowball	face	box	report

  leaf

train	France	**Go back 2 places.**	cow	sheep	calf

Go back 3 places.

minute	postman	country	**Go back to the start.**	blizzard	lake

hospital

Move forward 4 places.	blow	Lainey	family	**Finish**

Strand: Reading **Element:** Understanding LO 3
Strand: Writing **Element:** Understanding LO 3

Oral Genre **Communicating**

WALT: Gather information from the text and put it in order.

A Finish these sentence starters using information from the text.

- On February 24th...
- This is a report about...
- Many crops...
- The snow...
- The country was...
- At least 600...
- Temperatures...
- Local postmen...

- People were left...
- With nothing to heat...
- The locals from Lough Key...
- All traffic...
- Shops were without...
- Hospitals were...
- The blizzard of 1947 was...

B Roll a report! Retell the facts in the text in the correct order using these clues.

C Now, sort the information in the correct order.

1.	
2.	
3.	
4.	
5.	
6.	

A ✏️ **Plan a newspaper report using the information that you sorted on page 67.**

Weekend News Month: _____	Date: _____ Year: _____

Title: _____

Who: _____

What: _____

_____

_____

_____

Caption: _____

Where: _____

_____

When: _____

Caption: _____

Why: _____

_____

_____

_____

_____

_____

How: _____

_____

_____

_____

Strand: Writing **Element:** Exploring and Using LO 6, 7, 9

Tom Goes to China

WALT: Visualise; brainstorm; talk about our personalities.

 What does the title make you visualise?

A What do you know about China? Record some words in the spider diagram below. Use the prompt words to help you.

- food
- writing
- clothing
- people
- weather
- sport
- language
- art

FW

China

B 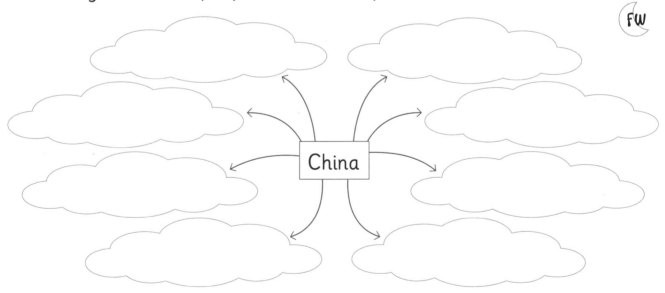 Look at the information below. If you were an animal, which would you be and why?

dragon	snake	horse	goat	monkey	rooster
dog	pig	rat	ox	tiger	rabbit

A Using the description below, draw an image of what happens during the Chinese Lantern Festival.

People go outside at night-time to look at the moon. They send up flying lanterns and fly bright drones. They have a meal and enjoy time together with family and friends.

B   Design a lantern using images described in the text.

The artwork on some lanterns shows traditional Chinese images and symbols such as fruit, flowers, birds, animals, people and buildings.

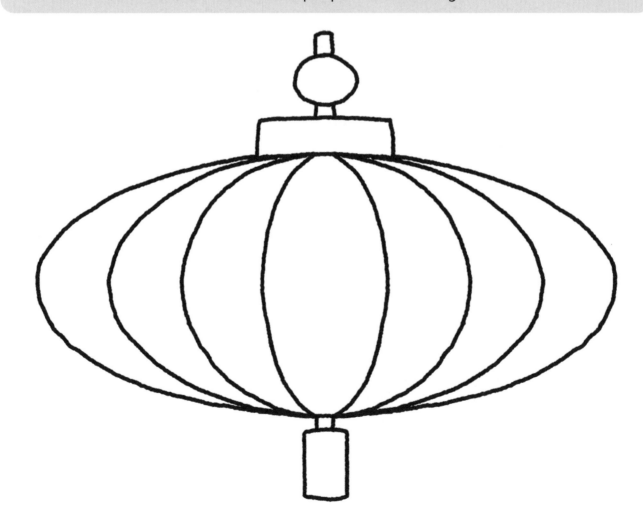

Strand: Oral Language **Element:** Exploring and Using LO 10

After Reading **Understanding**

WALT: Find words in the text with the same meaning as another word.

 A Word hunt: Find a word in the text with a similar meaning. Draw a picture to show its meaning.

moon: _____	lamp: _____	puzzles: _____
leaflet: _____	creatures: _____	sprinting: _____
carnival: _____	wicker: _____	vessel: _____
fowl: _____	buzz: _____	reward: _____

After Reading | **Comprehension**

WALT: Recall information about the text and give our own opinions; study words.

  Text detective

1. Why did Tom's family go to China?

2. Where did Tom get the information about the festivals?

3. How many lanterns are lit for the Lantern Festival?

4. What happened to the poet Qu Yuan?

5. What takes place on the fifth day of the fifth month?

6. Why do people hang special plants above their doors?

  Digging deeper: Discuss.

1. Recall a fact about China.

2. What does the saying 'this animal hides in your heart' mean?

3. Why do you think lantern owners write riddles on their lanterns?

4. Which festival would you like to see and why?

5. Look back to Unit 7, 'Pen Pals'. Can you make a connection between the traditions?

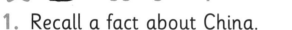 **Word study: Choose a bold word in the text and complete the following:** (fw)

1. Put it into a sentence.

2. Use it throughout the day.

3. Find smaller words within it.

4. Think of a word that has the same/opposite meaning.

Strand: Oral Language Elements: Understanding LO 5, 6; Exploring and Using LO 7
Strand: Reading Element: Exploring and Using LO 9
Strand: Writing Element: Understanding LO 4, 5

Say each word. Colour 'er' as you read it.

hammer	every	jersey	battery	flower	teacher	anger
painter	mother	brother	father	sister	mermaid	tower

B 🖊 Choose three 'er' words and write each in a sentence.

1. _____

2. _____

3. _____

 Say each word. Colour 'oi' as you read it.

coins	point	soil	disappoint	boil	noise	moist
voice	choice	avoid	toilet	spoil	poison	joint

D 🖍 Choose four 'oi' words and draw an image for each.

Adjectives are describing words.

  Use your senses to describe the images.

	Looks	Sounds	Feels	Tastes	Smells
🍿				salty	
🍉			slippery		
🌿		quiet			

WALT: Describe what we have read using words and symbols.

A Describe the Dragon Boat Festival using words, symbols or sentences.

B Match each piece of information to the correct festival.

It usually falls on a day between mid-January and mid-February.

People hang Chinese mugwort and calamus on their doors.

Chinese Lantern Festival

Billions of paper lanterns are lit during this festival.

According to an old saying, 'this animal hides in your heart'.

Chinese New Year

In China, each year is represented by one of 12 animals.

This festival marks the end of the Chinese New Year Festival.

Dragon Boat Festival

On the morning of the festival, every family eats *zongzi*.

Lantern owners write riddles on the lanterns.

Design a brochure about festivals in China using information in the text.

Title: _____

Classification (What is China?)

_____

Description (Describe each festival using important points.)

Chinese New Year

_____
_____
_____
_____

Chinese Lantern Festival

_____
_____
_____
_____

Dragon Boat Festival

_____
_____
_____
_____

Conclusion/Interesting point

_____

Picture Book | **Determining Importance**

WALT: Find important points in *The Magic Paintbrush* by Julia Donaldson.

Good readers look for important points while they read. This makes it easier to keep track of the main idea. When the story is complete, the important points will help you to retell the story.

  Record the important points in *The Magic Paintbrush*.

Page	Important point
	Shen is asked to go and catch some shrimp, fish and oysters.
	Shen makes pictures in the sand with a stick.
	There is a man sitting on a rock. He has a magic paintbrush.

Strand: Oral Language **Element:** Exploring and Using LO 8, 10
Strand: Reading **Element:** Exploring and Using LO 9

Spring Feasts

| Before Reading | Brainstorming |

 What words come to mind when you read the title?

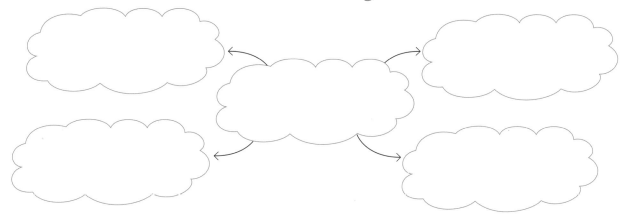

A **What do you know about each spring feast below? Write words or draw symbols.** (FW)

Saint Bridget's Day	
Shrove Tuesday	
Saint Valentine's Day	
Saint Patrick's Day	

B **Making connections: Have you ever watched a parade, made pancakes or sent a Valentine's card?**

My connection: _____

_____

A **Think of words to describe each person based on what you learn about them in the text.**

Character profile of Saint Bridget	Character profile of Saint Patrick

B ✏ **Write three important points about Shrove Tuesday.**

1. _____

_____

2. _____

_____

3. _____

_____

C 🖍 **Draw a pancake with your favourite toppings.**

Strand: Reading **Element:** Exploring and Using LO 7
Strand: Writing **Element:** Communicating LO 2

A **Write the story of Saint Bridget in the correct order.**

- She was sent to a bishop in Longford, who set up a house for her with some other girls.
- She was buried beside Saint Patrick's grave.
- Saint Bridget was born in County Louth.
- When she was a young girl, she heard Saint Patrick preaching.
- She noticed harps hanging on the walls.
- They told her that they were unable to play.
- They played music more beautiful than anyone had heard.
- She touched their fingers with her own.

1. _____

2. _____

_____

3. _____

_____

4. _____

5. _____

6. _____

7. _____

_____

8. _____

After Reading | **Comprehension**

WALT: Recall information about the text and give our own opinions; study words.

  Text detective

1. From a very early age, Bridget was known for her _____ .

2. Who was Bridget buried beside?

_____

3. What is Shrove Tuesday known as in France?

_____

4. On what date is Saint Valentine's Day?

_____

5. What did Patrick spend six years of his life doing?

_____

6. Why do people send cards to their loved ones on Saint Valentine's Day?

_____

  Digging deeper: Discuss.

1. How do you think Bridget made the harps play?

2. What do Christians do for Lent?

3. How did Judge Asterius put Valentine's faith to the test?

4. Do you think Patrick was happy to get sent back to Ireland?

5. Why do people make a Saint Bridget's cross? How is it made?

6. How did Patrick use the shamrock to explain Christianity?

 Word study: Choose a bold word in the text and complete the following:

1. Break it up into syllables (clap, click or tap).

2. Blend the word by dragging your finger along it quickly.

3. Write the word and colour the vowels blue and the consonants red.

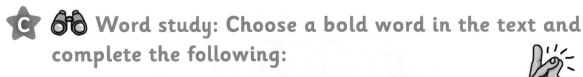

Strand: Oral Language **Elements:** Understanding LO 5, 6; Exploring and Using LO 7
Strand: Reading **Element:** Exploring and Using LO 9
Strand: Writing **Element:** Understanding LO 4

Phonics | **ou, or**

A 🖍 Say each word. Colour 'ou' as you read it.

group	soup	troupe	route	wound	would
should	could	cousin	country	rough	cough
couple	touch	croup	young	double	trouble

B Fill in the blanks using the correct 'ou' word above.

1. My _____ went to the cinema with my auntie.

2. Meg and Mel are in _____ with their mam.

3. The soldier had a _____, so he went to hospital.

4. Do not _____ the wet paint!

5. Have you ever travelled to a different _____?

C 🖍 Say each word. Colour 'or' as you read it.

sword	corn	born	north	sport	torch
fork	Cork	morning	form	doctor	short
storm	error	razor	record	anchor	porch

D ✏️ Fill in the blanks using the correct 'or' word above.

1. Red and white are the team colours of _____.

2. Baby Ed was _____ in springtime.

3. Lorraine drew the _____ straw.

4. "Can you please get me a knife and _____?" asked Lainey.

5. Dad cut his face with his _____ when he was shaving.

E 📓 In your copy, choose some 'ou' and 'or' words to put into sentences. Draw images to match the words.

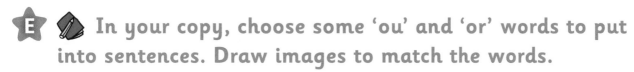

Remember: Adjectives are describing words.

  Describe each image using suitable adjectives.

shiny			
red			
smooth			

These adjectives are often used to describe food:

bitter	burnt	creamy	dull	fiery	fresh
gingery	milky	peppery	raw	rotten	savoury
sour	spicy	stale	strong	sugary	sweet
syrupy	tasteless	tasty	vinegary	yummy	zesty

 Complete each sentence using a suitable adjective.

1. The lemon was _____.

2. The bread was _____.

3. The curry was _____.

4. The chilli was _____.

5. The cupcake was _____.

6. The milk was _____.

7. The chicken was _____.

8. The toast was _____.

9. The salad was _____.

10. The soup was _____.

11. The chips were _____.

12. The onion was _____.

13. The sauce was _____.

14. The fish was _____.

Strand: Reading Element: Understanding LO 3
Strand: Writing Element: Understanding LO 3

A Freeze frame: Re-enact the scenes below.

The teacher will say 'freeze' and then tap one person from the group on the shoulder. They must describe the scene that they are in and what is happening.

- Valentine making the blind child see
- Patrick returning to Ireland as a priest
- Bridget in the king's castle
- Patrick getting captured
- Bridget as a young girl
- Valentine talking to the judge

B Hot seating: Write questions to ask each character.

C Roll and retell: Choose one of the people from the text to report on. Use the questions below to help you.

- Who are they?
- When did they live?
- What did they do?
- Where did they go?
- Why are they important?

Strand: Oral Language **Element:** Exploring and Using LO 11, 12
Strand: Writing **Element:** Communicating LO 2

Draft a report on one of the people in the text.

Who am I writing about?

_____

When were they born?

_____ AD

Where did they come from?

_____

What important things did they do?

_____

_____

_____

How are they remembered?

_____

_____

_____

Why did I enjoy learning about them?

_____

_____

_____

Strand: Writing **Elements:** Communicating LO 2; Exploring and Using LO 6, 7

Superman, my Superhero

Before Reading | **Brainstorming**

WALT: Imagine what we might do and describe what it would be like if we were superheroes.

 What are superheroes? What do they do? What do they wear? Describe the superheroes you know.

A Use the word boxes below to talk about superheroes.

Superhero key words		
identity	justice	powerful
costume	transform	brave
disguise	zoom	fast
cloak	whoosh	strong
mask	muscles	good
boots	climb	evil

Powers
flying
invisibility
X-ray vision
breathing ice
breathing fire
super strength

POW!

B If I were a Superhero... FW

My name would be:	My super powers would be:
_____	_____
I would look like:	_____
	_____
	I would fix these problems:
	_____
	_____
	_____

Strand: Oral Language **Element:** Exploring and Using LO 11, 12
Strand: Reading **Element:** Communicating LO 1

85

During Reading | **Book Talk**

WALT: Think about the thoughts and feelings of another person.

A Write what you think Christopher was thinking or feeling when...

1. He played the role of Superman.

_____

_____

_____

2. The horse began the third fence jump and suddenly stopped.

_____

_____

_____

3. He became a wheelchair user and needed a ventilator to breathe.

_____

_____

4. He began to move the index finger of his left hand.

_____

_____

B Why do you think the author chose to include this story in _Over the Moon?_

_____

_____

Strand: Oral Language **Element:** Exploring and Using LO 11
Strand: Reading **Elements:** Communicating LO 1; Exploring and Using LO 8

A Determining importance: Make up questions and answer them using information in the text. In your answers, think about what information is important and what is not important.

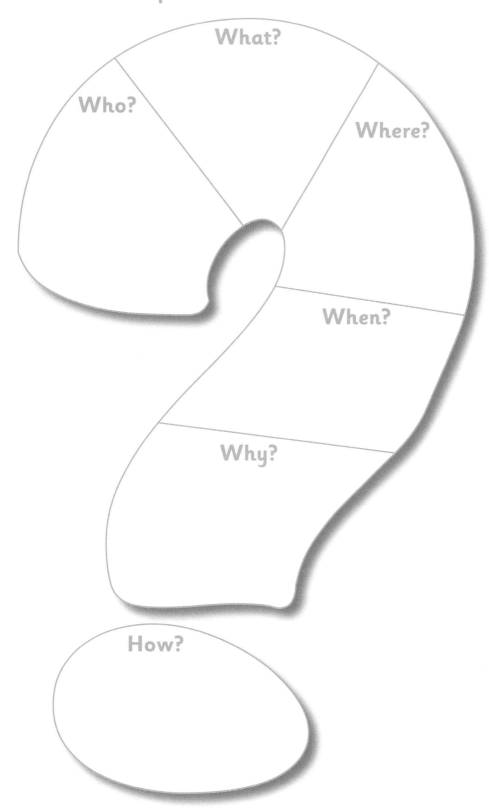

What?

Who?

Where?

When?

Why?

How?

After Reading | **Comprehension**

WALT: Recall information about the text and give our own opinions; explore phrases.

  A 🔍 **Text detective**

1. Which planet is Superman from?

2. What job did Clark get?

3. Who is Superman's enemy?

4. What did Christopher's horse do in the competition?

5. Which finger was Christopher able to move again?

6. What is a book about your life that you wrote yourself called?

  B 🎙 **Digging deeper: Discuss.**

1. Why do you think the Kents raised Clark as their own son?

2. Christopher played the role of a paralysed policeman before his accident. How might this have helped him after his own accident?

3. Why do you think Christopher was saying things like "get the gun" and "they're after us"?

4. How was Christopher like a superhero?

  C 🔭 **Phrase finder: Match each phrase to its meaning.**

1. a sneak peak	delighted
2. over the moon	it will take a long time
3. a long road	to see a little of what is to come

Strand: Oral Language **Elements:** Understanding LO 6; Exploring and Using LO 7, 10
Strand: Reading **Elements:** Understanding LO 6, Exploring and Using LO 9

A Say each word. Colour 'ey' as you read it.

keys	monkey	valley	chimney	hockey	kidney	honey
alley	donkey	jersey	journey	jockey	barley	money

B Ring the correct word in each sentence.

1. Evan and Tom play **hckey** / **hockey**.

2. Santa got stuck up the **chimney** / **chimnee**.

3. Mrs Lynch had a **kidney** / **kidnie** stone removed.

4. Christopher Reeve was a **jockey** / **joccey**.

5. Do you put **hooney** / **honey** on your pancakes?

C Read the rhyme. Colour 'ear' as you read it. Then, try to make up your own rhyme using 'ea' words.

Did you hear about the beard that disappeared and reappeared?

It made the dear man shed a tear and live in fear from year to year.

ear	earring	hear	appear
gear	weary	fear	disappear
clearly	beard	smear	year
tear	dear	spear	clear

D Ring 17 words that should take a capital letter and say why.

FW

superman is the only survivor of the planet krypton. jonathan and martha kent found him as a baby and brought him to their farm in smallville. to them, he looked human. the kents named the baby clark. as clark grew older, he found out that he had superpowers. he wanted to use them to help others. he helped people in danger and stopped bad things from happening. he got a job as a reporter for the *daily planet* after he wrote a story about superman.

A Imagine that you are the Kents. For each event below, write their thoughts and draw an image to create your own comic strip.

They found baby Clark.

They realised that he had superpowers.

He left home to study.

Lex Luthor was chasing him.

He saved people.

Strand: Oral Language **Element:** Exploring and Using LO 11, 12

A 🖊 Write a report on Christopher Reeve. Edit and proofread your work using your editing checklist.

Name: _____

Lived from _____ to _____

★ Most famous for _____

_____

Picture

Five facts

1. _____

_____

2. _____

_____

3. _____

_____

4. _____

_____

5. _____

_____

 B 👥 Swap your work with your partner. Give each other a star and a wish for your work.

(fw

Strand: Oral Language **Element:** Exploring and Using LO 11, 12
Strand: Writing **Element:** Exploring and Using LO 6, 7

91

Picture Book | **Questioning**

WALT: Ask questions about *We're All Wonders* by R. J. Palacio.

  A 🖊 What questions do you have about the story?

'I do ordinary things'

'I know I'm not an ordinary kid'

'I don't look ordinary'

We're All Wonders

'My mom says I'm unique'

'they'll see that I'm a wonder'

'People can change the way they see'

I wonder

_____

I wonder

_____

I wonder

_____

I wonder

_____

  B 🖊 What questions do you have for the author?

1. _____

2. _____

Strand: Reading **Element:** Exploring and Using LO 9
Strand: Writing **Element:** Understanding LO 3

The Witch's Lair

| Before Reading | Brainstorming |

WALT: Make predictions; visualise; make connections.

 What can you see, hear, smell, taste and touch when you read the title?

 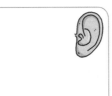   

A A lair is another word for a home or a den. What do you think a lair would look like? Draw, label and describe it.

B   Sneak preview: Read each snippet answer the questions.

Did you hear the news last week about the scouts who got lost when they went camping? Evan and I were there!

1. Can you make a text-to-self connection about getting lost?

This reminds me of a time when

We were supposed to tent up near the Ailwee Caves, but a thick yellow fog set in. The scout leaders found...

2. What do you predict will happen next?

I predict that

A 🖍 **Find words in the text that relate to spells. Write them on the cauldron.**

Double, double toil and trouble, fire burn and cauldron bubble.

B 👥 **Find action verbs in the text. Write them on the broomsticks.**

Examples: gather, place, stir, etc.

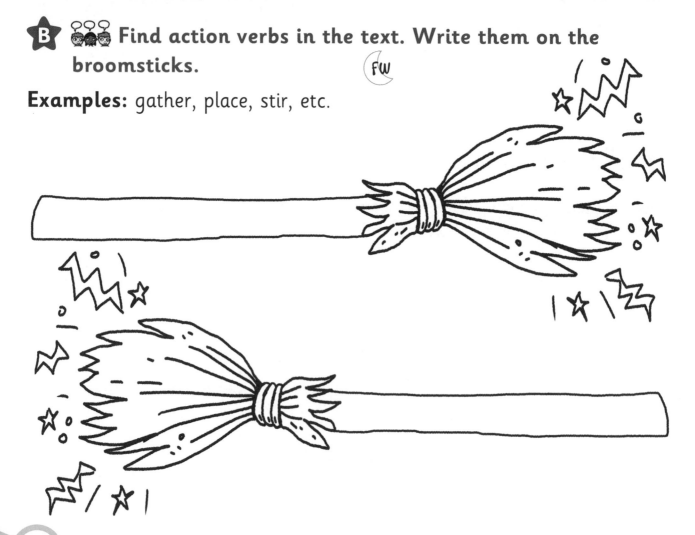

After Reading | **Understanding**

WALT: Find who, what, where, when, why and how in a text.

  A After they left the witch's lair, where did the children go and what did they do or see?

Where?	What?
Back through the lair	tiptoed
Back through	
Back around	
Back past	
Back to	
Into their	

B What do you predict will happen next and why?

1. The scout leaders will _____

2. The children _____

3. The witch _____

 C The witch's spell book contained another spell called 'How to turn a teacher into a goat'. What do you predict this spell involved?

After Reading | **Comprehension**

A **Text detective**

1. Where were the scouts supposed to tent up?

2. Why did they have to change the plan?

3. What happened when the scout leaders went to set up the lights?

4. What did the children find in the lair?

5. What did the children do?

6. How did Evan's phone help them?

B **Digging deeper: Discuss.**

1. Why do scouts go camping?

2. Why do you think the children did not listen to the scout leaders?

3. How do you think they felt when they realised they were in a witch's lair?

4. Why do you think the witch might want to look younger?

5. What do you think the witch would do if she saw the children?

6. What other spells might be in the spell book?

C **Word study: Choose a bold word in the text and complete the following:**

1. Read, cover, remember and spell it.

2. Write it three times.

3. Clap the syllables and then blend it.

4. Put it into a sentence.

Strand: Oral Language **Elements:** Understanding LO 5, 6; Exploring and Using LO 7
Strand: Reading **Element:** Exploring and Using LO 9
Strand: Writing **Element:** Understanding LO 4

A Say each word. Colour the silent 'h' as you read it.

heir	echo	while	whether	white	what	where	vehicle
why	hour	which	rhythm	honour	ghost	honest	exhibition

B Fill in the blanks using the correct silent 'h' word above.

1. Be _____ and tell us what happened.

2. Did you go to Miss Evelyn's art _____?

3. Can you clap the _____ of the song?

4. What would you do if you saw a _____?

5. Who is the _____ to the throne?

6. The mechanic repaired the _____.

C Say each word. Colour the silent 'c' as you read it. (Hint: A silent 'c' is found after the letter 's'.)

scene	scenery	science	scientist	descend	ascend	conscious
scent	muscles	scissors	crescent	disciple	abscess	conscience

D Cross out the nonsense words missing the silent 'c'.

scene	desend	sience	scientist
scent	cresent	descend	asend
science	muscles	ascend	scissors
scenery	crescent	disciple	conscious
disiple	abscess	senery	ascent
sissors	conscience	musles	absess

Examples of bossy verbs:

chop	catch	crouch	crack	cook	draw
drink	eat	explain	fetch	fill	flip
fly	fold	get	go	grill	mix
plug	pour	put	rest	roll	serve
slice	slide	sort	spread	stand	stick
throw	turn	use	undo	whisper	write

A 🖊 **Complete each sentence using a suitable bossy verb.**

1. _____ the onion in half. 2. _____ the jam on the bread.

3. _____ to your teacher. 4. _____ the rubbish in the bin.

5. _____ your clothes neatly. 6. _____ the secret in my ear.

7. _____ the die and play. 8. _____ the ingredients well.

9. _____ the child into a toad. 10. _____ the potion in one gulp.

B 🖊 **Ring the correct bossy verb in each sentence.**

1. "**Tidy / slice** your room," said Mum.

2. **Grill / listen** to your leader.

3. **Paint / bake** a picture of what you saw.

4. **Jump / mix** over the puddle.

5. **Close / slice** the door behind you.

6. **Throw / stand** the ball to Tom.

Strand: Reading **Element:** Understanding LO 3
Strand: Writing **Element:** Understanding LO 3

Spot eight differences between the pictures. Use present tense verbs to describe what you see and connectives to link your sentences.

Example: In the first picture, I **see**… **but** in the second picture, there **is**…

Plan and draft a procedure for the spell.

HOW TO TURN YOUR TEACHER INTO A GOAT

What do I need?

_____

_____

_____

_____

What must I do? (Use bossy verbs.)

Step 1: _____

Step 2: _____

Step 3: _____

Step 4: _____

Step 5: _____

Step 6: _____

Warning: Teacher might _____

Tip: To make the goat do what you say, add _____

Strand: Writing **Element:** Exploring and Using LO 6, 7

The 'How-to' Guide to Being Eight

Before Reading | **Brainstorming**

WALT: Ask and answer questions about our own lives.

 What words come to mind when you read the title?

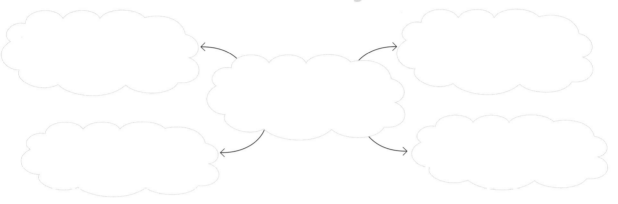

A Discuss the questions.

1. What are the best and worst things about being your age?

2. Since you started school, what has changed/stayed the same?

3. What things must you do now that you didn't have to do then?

4. What things can you still not do that you would like to do?

5. What advice would you give a child in Junior Infants?

6. Would you prefer to be a child or an adult? Why?

B Evan is going to give you some advice on being an eight-year-old. Write some of his thoughts.

During Reading | **Book Talk**

WALT: Find steps in the text; identify true and false statements.

A Record the steps required while you read.

How to dodge homework: _____

_____

_____

How to get off school: _____

_____

_____

How to get the toy you want: _____

_____

_____

B True or false?

Statement		True	False
1. When a builder comes home from work, they have to build a wall.		☐	☐
2. 'My dog ate my homework' is a good excuse.		☐	☐
3. You should keep to your story no matter what when telling a fib.		☐	☐
4. You should look tired, give your tummy a rub and get hot if you want a day off school.		☐	☐
5. If you put dots of your mam's mascara all over your face, she will take you to the doctor.		☐	☐
6. In the olden days, some children worked.		☐	☐

Strand: Oral Language **Element:** Communicating LO 1
Strand: Reading **Element:** Exploring and Using LO 7, 10
Strand: Writing **Element:** Exploring and Using LO 9

After Reading | Understanding

WALT: Think about adults' lives; design and caption a newspaper.

A Adults have a great life! Read this snippet from the text and tell them why you think they are lucky.

It's not fair that kids have to save up for something they want. If an adult wants something (like petrol or insurance), they can get it instantly by using their credit card. Grown-ups don't know how lucky they are!

Adults are lucky because _____

_____

B Think of your own excuses for not doing your homework.

(FW)

1. _____

2. _____

3. _____

4. _____

C The Tooth Fairy has found a stone instead of a tooth! Write a short newspaper report. Draw a picture and caption it.

Fairy Folk Times Business Edition

Headline: _____

_____

_____

_____

_____

_____

Strand: Oral Language **Element:** Communicating LO 1
Strand: Reading **Element:** Exploring and Using LO 7
Strand: Writing **Element:** Communicating LO 2

103

Text detective

1. What does Evan say it is tough being?

_____

2. What do eight-year-olds dislike doing?

_____

3. What might you get if you say you have a sore throat?

_____

4. How might you earn a few extra euro?

_____

5. How will teachers try to expose your fib?

_____

  Digging deeper: Discuss.

1. Why do you think Evan decided to write this guide?
2. Why do you think children do not like doing homework?
3. Can you make a connection to something in your own life?
4. What piece of advice in the text might not be good advice?
5. What kinds of fibs might people tell?
6. Why would it be easier to go to school than not?

  Phrase finder: Match each phrase to its meaning.

1. lucky ducks		it's not easy
2. the oldest trick in the book		people with good fortune
3. it's no walk in the park		a trick that has been used too often

Strand: Oral Language **Elements:** Understanding LO 6; Exploring and Using LO 7, 10
Strand: Reading **Elements:** Understanding LO 6; Exploring and Using LO 9

Phonics are, ear **Grammar** Bossy Verbs 2

A Read each word. Colour 'are' yellow. Colour 'ear' purple. Cover each word, spell it and then check it.

mare	hare	square	care	share	nightmare	rare
bare	dare	stare	fare	pare	parent	aware

bear	tear	wear	pearl	learn	earth

B Choose three 'are' and three 'ear' words and write each in a sentence.

1. _____

2. _____

3. _____

4. _____

5. _____

6. _____

Bossy verbs are used a lot in procedures.
Examples: cut, chop, stir

C Colour the bossy verbs in this procedure for making slime.

1. Mix ¼ cup of glue and ½ cup water in a bowl.

2. Add food colouring to the mixture and stir.

3. Pour ½ cup of borax solution into the mixture and stir. The slime will begin to form.

4. Stir the slime as much as you can and then knead it with your hands until it gets less sticky.

5. Store the slime in a plastic bag in the fridge.

A  Discuss what is happening in each picture. Act out each scene.

Strand: Oral Language **Elements:** Communicating LO 1; Exploring and Using LO 7

Writing Genre | **Exploring and Using**

WALT: Plan and draft a procedure.

 A Plan and draft one of the following procedures:

- How to get lots of sweets
- How to get in a teacher's good books

How to _____

Step 1: _____ _____ **Equipment:** _____ _____	**Illustration:**
Step 2: _____ _____ **Equipment:** _____ _____	**Illustration:**
Step 3: _____ _____ **Equipment:** _____ _____	**Illustration:**
Step 4: _____ _____ **Equipment:** _____ _____	**Illustration:**

Strand: Writing **Elements:** Communicating LO 2; Exploring and Using LO 6, 7

107

Which came first? How do you know?

The picture book *When I Grow Up* by Tim Minchin

Matilda the Musical

The film *Matilda*

Matilda by Roald Dahl

The song 'When I Grow Up'

Special edition *Matilda at 30*

 Clarifying makes things clear! Clarify what it means when the text says:

- 'the trees you get to climb when you're grown up'
- 'I will watch cartoons until my eyes go square'
- 'the heavy things you have to haul around'
- 'I'll play with things that Mum pretends that mums don't think are fun'

Lainey's Box of Delights

Before Reading	Brainstorming

 What can you see, hear, smell, taste and touch when you read the title? FW

 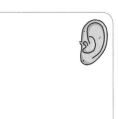   

A If you could have anything to eat now, what would it be?

My food wish: _____

B Word weaver: The words below appear in the text. Can you predict what the text might be about?

Masterchef	Nana	inspired	cakes	cheese	practise

My prediction: _____

C Use the illustrations to help you predict the steps in this recipe.

Step 1: _____

Step 2: _____

Step 3: _____

Step 4: _____

Step 5: _____

Step 6: _____

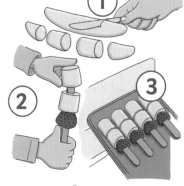

Strand: Oral Language **Element:** Exploring and Using LO 9
Strand: Reading **Element:** Exploring and Using LO 9

109

A   **Use the strategies in blue to help you complete the tasks.**

Visualising
Choose one recipe and draw the steps.

Questioning
Write two 'I wonder' questions about the story.

1. _____

_____

2. _____

_____

Making connections
What does this story remind you of?

_____

Predicting
What do you think Lainey will do between now and the competition?

_____

Determining Importance
Choose one recipe and pick out the key words

_____

_____

Clarifying
Was there anything that confused you?

_____

_____

Strand: Reading Elements: Understanding LO 2; Exploring and Using LO 9

WALT: Use time connectives; identify facts; use food vocabulary.

A Time connectives: Choose one of the recipes in the text and retell it using time connectives.

In the beginning		First of all	Firstly	Secondly
Thirdly	Then	Next	Later	After that
Afterwards	Eventually	Finally	Last of all	In the end

B List some of the food words in the text and draw an image of each.

Food word	Image	Food word	Image
strawberries			

Strand: Reading **Element:** Understanding LO 2
Strand: Writing **Elements:** Understanding LO 5; Exploring and Using LO 9

111

A **Text detective**

1. What has Lainey wanted to be since the age of four?

2. Who inspired Lainey to become a Junior Masterchef?

3. Where must the banana pops go for one hour?

4. What kind of water should you boil the asparagus in?

5. Why should you wash the potatoes?

B **Digging deeper: Discuss.**

1. What other method could you use to melt the chocolate?

2. Which recipe do you think is the healthiest and why?

3. What would happen if you skipped a step in a recipe?

4. What does Nana Smith mean when she says, "If at first you don't succeed, try, try and try again"?

5. Create a shopping list of the ingredients that you would need for the recipes.

6. Which recipe would be the easiest/hardest? Why?

C 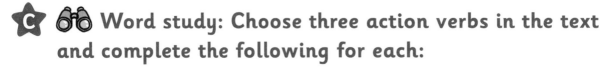 **Word study: Choose three action verbs in the text and complete the following for each:**

1. Draw a picture to show its meaning.

2. Write it three times using different colours.

3. Put it into a sentence to show its meaning.

Strand: Oral Language **Elements:** Understanding LO 5, 6; Exploring and Using LO 7
Strand: Reading **Elements:** Understanding LO 4; Exploring and Using LO 9

A Read each word. Colour 'ti' red. Colour 'si' blue. Clap and count the syllables.

nation	station	fiction	dictionary	education	patient
addition	relation	action	subtraction	question	solution

occasion	vision	revision	permission	explosion	invasion
division	erosion	decision	expression	extension	television

  B In your copy, make up rhymes using the words above.

Singular means one of something. **Plural** means more than one. Usually we add **s** to make a word plural, but some words are special. To change a word from singular to plural, we must look at its ending.

Examples:

If it ends in **ch**, **s**, **sh** or **x**, add **es** to make more than one.	beach → beach**es**, kiss → kiss**es**, wish → wish**es**, box → box**es**
If it ends in a consonant + **y**, drop **y** and add **ies** to make more than one.	jelly → jell**ies**, teddy → tedd**ies**, baby → bab**ies**, cherry → cherr**ies**

 C Roll a die. When you land on a word, say whether we add 's', 'es' or 'ies' to change it to plural. (FW)

A Use the illustrations to discuss the steps in this procedure. Then, fill in the steps in the correct order.

- Place the pot in a sunny spot and wait.
- Give the seed a drink using the watering can.
- Tip some compost into the pot and press it down.
- Cover the seed with compost and pat it gently.
- Place a seed in the hole.
- Scoop out a hole in the compost using the trowel.

Sunflower seeds are yummy to eat and fun to grow!

How to Plant a Seed

What you will need:

seeds	compost	plant pot	trowel	watering can

1. _____

2. _____

3. _____

4. _____

5. _____

6. _____

Strand: Oral Language **Element:** Exploring and Using LO 9

Writing Genre | **Exploring and Using**

WALT: Write a procedure using time connectives and action verbs.

 A 👥 Choose your favourite recipe. Talk through the steps with your partner. Record it using time connectives and action verbs.

fw

Examples of action verbs:

grate	blend	layer	level	melt	simmer	scramble
spread	stir	slice	taste	cut	pour	bake
serve	grill	add	boil	fry	chop	dip

Recipe for _____

Ingredients:

_____

_____

_____

Method:

Step 1: _____

_____

_____

Step 2: _____

_____

_____

Step 3: _____

_____

_____

Step 4: _____

_____

_____

Picture Book | **Clarifying**

WALT: Clarify phrases in *Sammy and the Skyscraper Sandwich* by Lorraine Frasier.

Good readers clarify things while they read. If you do not understand a word, you might need to look it up in the dictionary or online.

A 🖊 **Can you clarify each of the underlined words or phrases?**

1. a <u>skyscraper</u>

2. a <u>comb</u> of honey

3. <u>Swiss</u> cheese

4. <u>grated</u> carrot

5. <u>crisp</u> lettuce

6. a <u>sprig</u> of parsley

B 🖊 **Answer the questions.**

1. What time of year is it? How do you know?

2. What is on the kitchen table? How does this relate to the title?

3. How is Sammy travelling up through the house?

4. What creatures can you see in the book?

5. Are Sammy's family musical? How do you know?

6. What did Sammy think he was really making?

Strand: Oral Language **Element:** Understanding LO 6
Strand: Reading **Element:** Exploring and Using LO 9

The Teachers' Surprise

Before Reading	Brainstorming

WALT: Talk about our emotions and events in our lives.

✏️ **What does the title make you visualise?**

⭐ A ✏️ **How is your mindfulness journey going? Tick the emotions you have felt. Discuss.** (FW)

bored ☐	surprised ☐	shocked ☐	jealous ☐	sad ☐
happy ☐	confident ☐	enraged ☐	confused ☐	shy ☐
angry ☐	mischievous ☐	lonely ☐	excited ☐	smug ☐

⭐ B 👥 **Write a sentence about a memory of an emotion that you have felt. Discuss.**

I felt _____ when _____

_____

⭐ C 👥 **What was the best surprise you ever got? Why?**

_____

_____

_____

_____

_____

A Hot seating: Imagine that you are Tom and Ella standing at the school gate. Record what you are seeing and thinking.

FW

B Clarifying: Two clues in the text suggest that the parents knew about the surprise. Find them and record them below.

Page no.	Evidence

Strand: Reading **Element:** Communicating LO 1

After Reading | **Understanding**

WALT: Be creative with language by drawing what we see while we read.

A **Visualising: Read each snippet from the text and draw what you see in your mind.**

The birds were chirping, the sun was waking up and the flowers were blooming.	
His dog Luna whined as he closed the front gate.	
Ella devoured a bowl of warm porridge and gulped down a glass of freshly squeezed orange juice (with bits).	
The car park was full to the brim...	
The entire school erupted with laughter.	

After Reading | **Comprehension**   **WALT:** Recall information about the text and give our own opinions; explore phrases.

Ⓐ 🔍 Text detective

1. What did Tom want to be when he grew up?

_____

2. What did Tom think his mam got wrong?

_____

3. How did Tom's dog, Luna, react to him leaving for school?

_____

4. Where did Ella go with her family at the weekend?

_____

4. Who arrived to collect the children and what were they wearing?

_____

Ⓑ ⚒ Digging deeper: Discuss.

1. Why do you think Tom did not want to go to school?

2. What kind of a person is Ella? How do you know?

3. Why do you think some vehicles have logos on them?

4. Why were the children surprised to see Mrs Lynch dressed up?

5. How was Tom's morning different to Ella's up until they met at the school gate?

6. How did the author create suspense in this story?

Ⓒ 👀 Phrase finder: Complete each sentence with a suitable phrase from the story.

1. People come in _____.

2. Emma's shopping trolley was _____.

3. "Let's _____," said Dad, as he put on his hiking boots.

4. Nana knew the recipe like the _____.

Strand: Oral Language **Elements:** Understanding LO 6; Exploring and Using LO 7, 10
Strand: Reading **Elements:** Understanding LO 6; Exploring and Using LO 9

Phonics ei, o

A **Read each word. Colour 'ei' as you read it.**

reins	veil	height	receive	eight	eighteen	eighty
beige	vein	ceiling	leisure	neigh	neighbour	weigh

B **Fill in the blanks using the correct 'ei' word above.**

1. The colour of the scouts' uniform is _____.

2. I like to read at my _____.

3. The nurse stuck a needle into my _____.

4. My _____ looked after my dog when I was on holidays.

5. I have 82 cent, so I need _____ cent more to make a euro.

6. The sound that a horse makes is a _____. FW

7. Christopher Reeve got tangled in his horse's _____.

C **Read each word. Colour 'o' as you read it.**

some	front	gloves	another	dozen	somebody	nothing
love	son	other	brother	mother	monkey	Monday

D **Ring the correct word in each sentence.**

1. My brother is my dad's **sun** / **son**.

2. Can I have **anuther** / **another** cake, please?

3. Tom and Ella stood at the **frunt** / **front** gate.

4. "**Somebody** / **sumebody** is giving us a surprise," said Lainey.

5. The **monkey** / **munkey** swung from branch to branch.

6. The teachers wore big **gloves** / **gluves** for the sumo wrestling.

7. Nana bought a **duzen** / **dozen** eggs for baking cakes.

Tired words are words that get used a lot in our writing. If we use the same words over and over again, it can sound boring. Some examples of words that are overused are '**happy**', '**nice**' and '**bad**'.

A ✏ **Put tired words to bed! Match the words that you could use instead of these words to each of the tired words.**

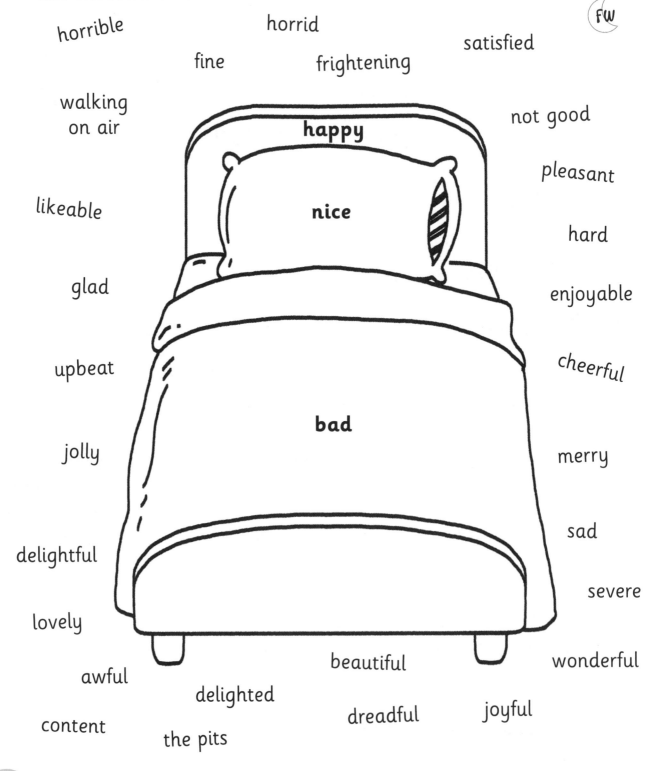

horrible

horrid

satisfied

fine   frightening

FW

walking
on air

not good

happy

pleasant

likeable

nice

hard

glad

enjoyable

upbeat

cheerful

bad

jolly

merry

sad

delightful

severe

lovely

beautiful   wonderful

awful

delighted   joyful

dreadful

content

the pits

Strand: Reading **Element:** Understanding LO 3
Strand: Writing **Element:** Understanding LO 3

Retell the story of 'The Teachers' Surprise' using the images and sentence starters below.

 Story Map: The Teachers' Surprise

In the beginning...

In the middle...

At the end...

A **Create a character for a story using the prompts below.**

Prompts	
Gender: girl or boy	
Name and surname	
Age: young or old	
Where they are from	
Appearance: What do they look like/what do they wear?	
Personality: What are they like?	

B **Create a setting for a story using the prompts below.**

Prompts	
City or countryside	
Name of the place	
Indoors or outdoors	
Describe the scene	
Day or night	
Write a description	
What is in the background or foreground?	
Does the setting change in your story or stay the same?	

Strand: Writing **Elements:** Communicating LO 1, 2; Exploring and Using LO 6, 7

The Day the School Stood Still

Before Reading | **Brainstorming**

 What words come to mind when you read the title?

A Discuss the story title using the strategies below.

Questioning	Predicting	Connecting	Clarifying
Can you turn the title into a question?	Make a prediction about the story from reading the title.	Make a connection to a time when you stood still.	How can a building 'stand still'? Is it not always still?

B Word weaver: The words below appear in the text. Can you predict what it will be about?

newbie	nervous	unusual	glasses	traits
teacher	leaving	cool	surprise	modern-day

C  Record your personal prediction about the text.

- Compare your prediction with your partner's. How are they different?
- Ask your partner to explain how they came up with their prediction.

During Reading | **Book Talk**

WALT: Stand in the shoes of a character; find evidence in the text.

A **Read each snippet from the text and answer the questions.**

 **(Stop at page 137.)** On Newbie Eve – the evening before the newbie arrived – Lainey lay tossing and turning in her bed. What would her new teacher be like?

1. What was Lainey thinking? Record the questions that were running through her mind.

(a) _____

(b) _____

(c) _____

 **(Stop at page 138.)** Lainey was on the edge of her seat, tapping her pencil against the table.

2. What happened next? How did the children react?

_____

_____

 **(Stop at page 139.)** You probably think you already know all there is to know about witches, but you don't.

3. Can you clarify what is meant by the sentence above?

_____

_____

Strand: Oral Language **Element:** Exploring and Using LO 9
Strand: Reading **Element:** Communicating LO 1

After Reading | **Understanding**

A Discuss and record a question that you have about the story and a question that you have for the author.

_____

_____

_____

_____

_____

_____

B Complete the story map.

How does the story begin?

What is the setting?

Who are the characters?

How was Lainey feeling about the arrival of the newbie?

How did the children react when they saw their new teacher?

How does the story end?

What will happen next?

What is the author's message?

What was unusual about Ms Grant?

fw

What surprised or confused you?

WALT: Recall information about the text and give our own opinions; explore phrases.

A Text detective

1. Describe the rain in Kerrypike.

2. Where did Ms Carol go?

3. Name the three places you might have seen a witch.

4. What do witch teachers hate?

5. How did the children know that Ms Grant was a witch?

6. Which other story in this book does this one remind you of? Why?

B Digging deeper: Discuss.

1. How would you describe Lainey's personality?

2. Why do you think she was tapping her pencil?

3. Why do you think a witch teacher would want to 'blend in'?

4. What do you think 'eyes at the back of their heads' means?

5. Why did the author choose the poem 'Saw my Teacher on a Saturday' to go with this story?

C Phrase finder: Match each phrase to its meaning.

1. soaked to the bone		annoys them
2. tossing and turning		drenched
3. gets their goat		not able to relax

Strand: Oral Language **Elements:** Understanding LO 6; Exploring and Using LO 7, 10
Strand: Reading **Elements:** Understanding LO 6; Exploring and Using LO 9

| Phonics | ure, ie | Grammar | Speech Marks |

WALT: Explore 'ure' and 'ie' words; use speech marks.

A 🖍 Say each word. Colour 'ure' red and 'ie' green. Clap and count the syllables.

future	adventure	capture	puncture	fracture	furniture
nature	moisture	picture	posture	creature	departure

field	piece	chief	shield	shriek	movie	priest
tier	thief	grief	yield	brief	belief	retrieve

B ✏ Choose three 'ure' and three 'ie' words and write each in a sentence.

1. _____

2. _____

3. _____

4. _____

5. _____

6. _____

We use **speech marks** to show what someone is saying.
Example:
"It's so boring staying inside, Mum," she said in a fed-up voice.

C ✏ Insert speech marks where appropriate.

1. I can't find my glasses, said the teacher in a panic.

2. A stitch in time saves nine, Nana Smith remarked.

3. I cannot believe what I am hearing, stated Mam.

4. Lainey, would you pass me my book, please? asked Ms Grant.

5. Go straight ahead and turn left, Grandad told the new teacher.

A narrative needs to have a beginning, a middle and an ending. It should have a catchy title that makes you want to find out what the story is about. A good story should also have exciting parts that make you want to read on.

A **Think of some fairy tales that you know. Retell them using the framework below.**

Examples: Little Red Riding Hood, Hansel and Gretel

Beginning	Middle	Ending
▪ Once upon a time there was… ▪ One day…	▪ But then… ▪ The next thing that happened was…	▪ At last… ▪ In the end… ▪ The final thing…

B **Below are some catchy titles. Can you think of four more?**

The Tale of Whispering Woods

The Mysterious Neighbours in Number 33

Under the Floorboards

1. _____

2. _____

3. _____

4. _____

C **Setting the scene: What happened next? Create some stories with your partner.**

1. Lainey was alone in the house. There was a knock at the door.

2. Baby Ed was playing in the kitchen. There was a loud crash.

3. He hopped over the gate. The dog began to growl.

4. She hid behind a tree and changed into her disguise.

5. Evan went to feed his pet snake. He looked in the cage. It wasn't there!

Strand: Oral Language **Elements:** Communicating LO 2; Exploring and Using LO 9

Writing Genre | **Exploring and Using**

WALT: Create a story plan; discuss our work with others.

 A What happened next? Plan the next chapter in the story.

The story of 'The Day the School Stood Still' is not complete. We do not know what Ms Grant got up to or what happened to the children. Imagine that you are a pupil in Ms Grant's class. Tell the events from your point of view.

Story Mountain

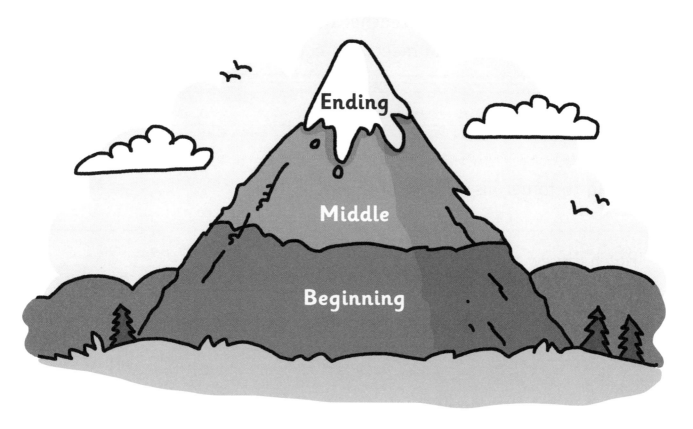

 B In your copy, draft your story. Try to use some of the words and phrases that you learned from the text.

 C Swap stories with your partner. Give opinions on your partner's work using the prompts below.

- I like the way you…
- I am wondering why you…?
- I like way you described…
- I like this word/phrase…

- I was confused by…
- I found… interesting/ surprising/ shocking, because…

Strand: Oral Language **Element:** Communicating LO 2
Strand: Writing **Elements:** Communicating LO 1; Exploring and Using LO 6, 7

131

Good readers read between the lines as they read. They look for a message that the author was trying to send even though they may not have written it. This is called inferring.

A ✏️ **Read between the lines. What do you infer from each of the following parts of the story?** (FW

1. When Bobby runs into his teacher outside of school, he learns that there is more to her than meets the eye.

_____

_____

_____

2. 'trying to forget his teacher problems'

_____

3. 'But he knew that would only make things worse.'

_____

4. 'There was an awkward silence.'

_____

5. 'Those ducks sure do like you.'

_____

6. 'But they were ready to say goodbye.'

_____

7. Is Ms Kirby still a monster?

_____

_____

_____

_____

Strand: Oral Language **Element:** Exploring and Using LO 9
Strand: Reading **Element:** Exploring and Using LO 9
Strand: Writing **Element:** Communicating LO 1

The Mysterious House

Before Reading	Brainstorming

WALT: Brainstorm; prepare sentences before I write them.

 What words come to mind when you read the title?

 A **Prepare a sentence about this story using a prediction about the title.**

My prediction: _____

_____

B **Read the snippet below. Prepare a sentence that shows what you see in your mind.**

It was surrounded by laurel hedging. The grass was wild and long. The house was so rundown that it looked as if a strong wind could blow it down.

This is what I can see, touch, smell, hear and taste when I visualise 'The Mysterious House':

A 🖍 **Visualising: Highlight the vocabulary in each sentence that helps you to visualise the scene.**

The sun was splitting the stones. The sky was blue, with not a whisper of cloud.

The grass was wild and long. The house was so rundown that it looked as if a strong wind could blow it down.

Tom trudged over to the house and placed his trembling hand on the old wooden gate.

Making connections: Prepare before you write.

1. Does this story remind you of another story in the reader?

_____

2. Does it remind you of anything else?

_____

 Visualise: Highlight the words that make you see the images. Draw what you see.

> There in the grass was a row of tiny houses, slightly bigger than matchboxes. Tiny wisps of smoke piped from the chimneys and faint lights shone from the windows. In front of the houses was a street. It was hustling and bustling with activity. Little people with wings were busy going about their business.

 Prepare and write two questions to ask the fairy villagers. FW

1. _____

2. _____

 Clarifying: What did it mean when the text said...

1. 'kids will be kids'?

_____

2. 'as lonely as a goldfish in a bowl'?

_____

After Reading | **Comprehension**

WALT: Recall information about the text and give our own opinions; explore phrases.

  Text detective

1. What was the weather like that day?

2. Why was Tom afraid to retrieve his ball?

3. What was Miss Teary counting in the garden?

4. Where will Tom go tomorrow and what will he do there?

5. What happened the last time a child had entered Miss Teary's garden?

B **Digging deeper: Discuss.**

1. Why did people think that Miss Teary was a witch or a ghost?

2. What is interesting about Miss Teary's name?

3. How do you think Tom felt when she was shouting at him?

4. Why do you think the fairies chose this garden to live in?

5. What does the phrase 'took his breath away' mean?

6. How might things not always appear as they seem?

C **Phrase finder: Draw a picture for each phrase.**

the sun was splitting the stones	standing as still as a statue	as fast as a greyhound

Strand: Oral Language **Elements:** Understanding LO 6; Exploring and Using LO 7, 10
Strand: Reading **Elements:** Understanding LO 6; Exploring and Using LO 9

Phonics ore, le   Grammar   Capital Letters 4

WALT: Explore 'ore' and 'le' words; use capital letters and full stops.

  A Say each word. Colour 'ore' as you read it.

chore	wore	more	core	bored	folklore	snore	store
score	tore	pore	sore	shore	seashore	before	adore

 B Fill in the blanks using the correct 'ore' word above.

1. I thought fairies were just _____.

2. Baby Ed tried to eat an apple _____!

3. Evan has a _____ abscess in his mouth.

4. Tom was _____, so he played with the ball.

5. Have you heard how loudly my dad can _____?

  C Say each word. Colour 'le' as you read it.

able	bottle	couple	giggle	buckle	dazzle	castle	cattle
stable	bangle	double	cuddle	beetle	Google	middle	circle

  D Ring the correct word in each sentence.

1. Baby Ed has a lovely **giggle / giggel**.

2. Meg and Mel are **duble / double** trouble.

3. The fairies gathered round in a **curcel / circle**.

4. "Can you fasten my belt **buckle / buckel**, please?" asked Tom.

5. Miss Evelyn wore a pretty **bangel / bangle** on her wrist.

  E Ring the missing capital letters and full stops.

despite being at least 150 years old, she was as fast as a greyhound

within seconds, she was upon him

tom closed his eyes, waiting to be turned into a frog, a slug or another slimy creature he braced himself, but nothing came

Oral Genre **Communicating**

WALT: Examine character traits and draw a portrait of a character.

 A Tom is the main character in the story. Discuss the questions in this character profile and record your ideas.

What was Tom's problem?	What do you know about Tom?
How did he solve the problem?	
What were his character traits?	How did Tom's character change over time?

B In your copy, draw a portrait of Miss Teary. Highlight the words that helped you to make the images. (FW)

Miss Teary was ancient. Her face was very crinkly, like someone had taken a photo of the world's oldest person and squashed it tight before unfolding the paper – so deep were her wrinkles.

Strand: Oral Language **Element:** Understanding LO 5
Strand: Writing **Element:** Exploring and Using LO 8

A Write your own story using the prompts below to help you.

| **Beginning** Introduce the characters and the setting. | It was a windy afternoon in Clonakilty. Lainey and her mam decided to drive to the beach to fly a kite. As soon as they arrived, Lainey jumped out of the car and ran down to the seashore. In no time at all, her kite was soaring high in the sky. |

| **Middle** What is the problem? | As she raced along the shoreline, she looked over her shoulder. Suddenly, something caught her eye. _____ _____ _____ _____ |

| **Ending** How is the problem solved? | _____ _____ _____ _____ _____ _____ |

B Respond to your partner's work. Give your opinions using the prompts below.

- I like the way you...
- I am wondering why you...?
- I like way you described...
- I like this word/phrase...

- I was confused by...
- I found... interesting/surprising/ shocking, because...

Picture Book | **Inferring**

WALT: Use the strategy of inferring with *Rose Meets Mr Wintergarten* by Bob Graham.

A ✏️ **Read between the lines. What do you infer from each of the following parts of the story?**

1. 'they felt at home'

_____

_____

2. 'The sun never touched the house next door.'

_____

_____

3. 'Next door everything bristled.'

_____

_____

4. 'There were stories in the street about Mr Wintergarten.'

_____

_____

5. 'She twisted her fingers in her handkerchief.'

_____

_____

6. 'His dinner was cold, grey and uninviting'

_____

_____

7. 'Mr Wintergarten opened his curtains.'

_____

_____

8. 'He saw Rose's ball and thoughtfully pushed it with his toe.'

_____

_____

Strand: Reading **Element:** Exploring and Using LO 9